"Stay with me tonight, Cody. Sleep with me."

She saw the hesitation in his eyes. She knew that if he spoke, he'd turn her down. That wasn't an option.

"One night, tonight. Let's pretend we are strangers, that we've never met before, that we saw each other in the club and started to dance," she said, hoping he didn't notice the hint of desperation in her voice.

A small smile touched Cody's mouth but didn't reach his eyes. "Once we do this, Tinsley, we can't go back."

"When dawn breaks this will all be a dream. And everything will be as it was before."

"You're naive if you think that," Cody told her, his voice rough.

"I want you, Cody," Tinsley insisted. "One night of pleasure, no expectations, and no demands."

"Are you sure about this?" Cody demanded.

No, not at all.

But she was going to do it anyway.

* * *

Wrong Brother, Right Kiss by Joss Wood
is part of the Dynasties: DNA Dilemma series.

DYNASTIES

Will the results of one DNA test upend everything for this American blue blood family?
Don't miss a single twist or turn!

Secrets of a Bad Reputation
Wrong Brother, Right Kiss
Lost and Found Heir
The Secret Heir Returns

Dear Reader,

Welcome to book two of the DNA Dilemma series and the luxurious world of the Ryder-Whites!

Callum Ryder-White is still causing problems for the rest of the Ryder-White clan. His obsession with their DNA results and who owns his dead brother's stake in Ryder International is driving them all mad.

Tinsley Ryder-White, along with her sister, Kinga (*Secrets of a Bad Reputation*), heads up Ryder International's PR division and is very busy organizing functions to celebrate Ryder International's one hundredth year in business. She's also still recovering from her divorce of JT Gallant, whom she met when she was fifteen. She thought they'd be together forever.

Tinsley has always had a prickly relationship with JT's older brother, Cody Gallant, the owner of a successful international events company. Cody never supported their marriage and even went so far as to ask her not to marry his brother.

But, strangely, Tinsley finds herself seeing in the new year with Cody, naked! And that's not the only consequence of their hookup...

Happy reading!

Joss

xxx

Connect with me on Facebook at JossWoodAuthor, Twitter @JossWoodbooks, Bookbub at joss-wood and josswoodbooks.com.

JOSS WOOD

———

WRONG BROTHER, RIGHT KISS

HARLEQUIN®
DESIRE™

Recycling programs
for this product may
not exist in your area.

ISBN-13: 978-1-335-73554-6

Wrong Brother, Right Kiss

Copyright © 2022 by Joss Wood

This edition published by arrangement with Harlequin Books S.A.

For questions and comments about the quality of this book, please contact us at CustomerService@Harlequin.com.

Harlequin Enterprises ULC
22 Adelaide St. West, 41st Floor
Toronto, Ontario M5H 4E3, Canada
www.Harlequin.com

Printed in U.S.A.

Joss Wood loves books, coffee and traveling—especially to the wild places of southern Africa and, well, anywhere. She's a wife and a mom to two young adults. She's also a slave to two cats and a dog the size of a small cow. After a career in local economic development and business, Joss writes full-time from her home in KwaZulu-Natal, South Africa.

Books by Joss Wood

Harlequin Desire

Dynasties: DNA Dilemma

Secrets of a Bad Reputation
Wrong Brother, Right Kiss

Murphy International

One Little Indiscretion
Temptation at His Door
Back in His Ex's Bed

Harlequin Presents

South Africa's Scandalous Billionaires

How to Undo the Proud Billionaire
How to Win the Wild Billionaire

Visit her Author Profile page at Harlequin.com, or josswoodbooks.com, for more titles.

You can also find Joss Wood on Facebook, along with other Harlequin Desire authors, at Facebook.com/harlequindesireauthors!

Prologue

Tinsley Ryder-White adored her grandfather's study, the vast collection of books sitting on the floor-to-ceiling shelves. She was seven years old and she loved nothing better than to crawl under his enormous desk, tuck herself into the corner and hide out from the world.

It was the summer holidays, and nobody would look for her here and she'd be left alone for a few hours...*yay*!

Tinsley tucked a cushion behind her back and flipped open the cover of her book, sighing with pleasure. Reading was her favorite thing in the whole wide world.

She hadn't gotten past page three when she heard the heavy door to the study open and her heart leaped into her chest. Her grandfather was back and when he found her, she'd be in a heap of trouble.

Tinsley froze and prayed that Callum—he wouldn't allow them to call him anything but his first name—didn't sit down and stretch out his legs. If he did that, she'd be discovered.

It was a grown-up game of hide-and-seek. She just had to stay still and keep very, very quiet.

"Good morning, Callum," Daddy said, and Tinsley had to slap her hand across her mouth to smother her squeak. She'd thought Daddy and Callum had left for work already... Man, why hadn't she checked?

"Don't bother sitting down—this won't take long," Callum said, sounding cross. Then again, Callum always sounded cross.

Tinsley held her breath and buried her face in her hands.

If they found her, she was toast.

"I met with my lawyer yesterday and updated my will."

"Let me guess. I'm not in it," Daddy said, sounding tired.

"Au contraire. Since I have no other male heir, I have little choice but to leave everything to you," Callum responded, sounding angrier than she'd ever heard him. "But I placed a provision in the document that if I find another male heir, anyone with a close connection to me—but not to Benjamin—he shall inherit my thirty percent share of Ryder International, all my properties and my financial assets."

"I knew you disliked me, Callum, but I never realized you hated me this much." Daddy sounded like someone was choking him.

"I told you not to take Benjamin's side, that there would be consequences if you defied me. The only silver lining to Benjamin being homosexual is that he wouldn't have sired any children."

"Jesus, Callum, you can't say stuff like that. Your brother didn't want to marry a woman—he wanted to be with Carlo. I just supported his wish to live his life the way he wanted."

"And your support gave him the courage to tell the world he was gay and to move in with that man! He probably left his share of Ryder International to him, someone with no connection to us!"

"Firstly, as I've told you before, there's no proof he left his shares to Carlo and if he did, why would Carlo hide his identity behind a blind trust? And I was in my early twenties when all this happened and even if I had discussed his will with him, which I didn't, I would've had no influence over him! Like you, Ben made his own decisions. You are punishing me for something Ben did and that's not fair."

"Life's not fair, boyo. Haven't you realized that yet?" Callum demanded.

"What about Kinga and Tinsley?" Daddy asked and Tinsley's eyes widened at the sound of her name.

"What about them?"

"They, like me, carry the Ryder-White name, the

only heirs who do. You could leave everything to them—they carry your genes."

"They are silly girls. Ryder-White males carry the name, the genes, the blood." Callum's voice was low and nasty. "Your daughters are beneath my notice. I have no interest in them. But, do not doubt me on this, if they put a foot out of line and tarnish the Ryder-White name, if they are anything less than perfect, *you* will bear the consequences, James.

"You and your family live here, at Ryder's Rest, because I allow it. You are paid an overinflated salary because I choose to give you that money. You certainly are not worth it. Your lifestyle depends on my generosity. I gave you everything and I can take it all away. Make sure your family understands that you live in my house, under my rules."

Callum was horrible, Tinsley thought. A part of her wanted to scramble out from under the desk and kick his shins and scream at him for being nasty to her dad but another part of her was scared, terrified, actually.

Because, as he said, if she stepped out of line, bad things would happen.

One

Six weeks ago

Well, hello to the New Year.

Tinsley Ryder looked down from the balcony of the newest Ryder International bar and watched a dark-haired man spin his blond partner and dip her over his arm. She laughed with delight and gave him the look that suggested he'd get lucky later. Tinsley wrenched her eyes off them and stroked the skin on the ring finger of her left hand. She'd removed her engagement and wedding rings two years ago—six months after their divorce—but despite so much time passing, she still missed JT.

Correction, she didn't miss her husband; she missed being married, being half of a whole. She missed sex and having someone to talk to at the end of the day.

For nearly half her life, she'd seen in the New Year with JT and the memories—counting down the clock while standing in San Marco Square, watching the ball fall in Times Square or while holed up in a cabin in Aspen—bombarded her. This was the second New Year she'd seen in solo and, honestly, it sucked.

JT had someone new, but she, well…she was *still* coming to terms with the death of their marriage and the dreams she'd made, the life she'd planned. She could still accurately remember the details of the forever house she'd designed, recalled the names she'd decided on for the three kids she wanted, could recite the itineraries of future holidays.

Planned and perfect.

Yet her flawless life fell apart when JT up and left her and moved to Hong Kong, just as his brother had predicted all those years ago.

Despite knowing that five minutes had passed since the countdown, Tinsley looked at her watch again. She wished she could leave and return to her hotel room just a block away, but this was the opening of their newest bar and it was her job, as cohead of publicity for Ryder International, to be here.

Ryder International opened one or two new bars a year and the preparations took up to two years from conception to implementation. Ryder employed various teams to get the new bar up and running but it was her job to ensure the new venue received the maximum amount of publicity. To achieve that, she contracted Gallant Events to stage an opening night that would wow the celebrities and influencers and make the bar the hottest, coolest spot in the city.

Her publicity team and Cody Gallant's event team had worked together on four other opening nights. They were exceedingly good at their jobs. Tinsley always flew in a week before opening night, and she knew both teams—hers and Cody's—dreaded her arrival as she came with a million questions and another million demands. She saw the eye rolls, heard the frustration in their voices and reminded herself that it was her job to provide perfection.

It was what Ryder International was known for and perfection was what she delivered.

Kinga was equally dedicated to the pursuit of perfection, a good thing since they ran the PR department together. They did, however, have distinctly separate responsibilities and Tinsley was glad that she wasn't running point on organizing Ryder's very exclusive Valentine's Day Ball. Especially since Callum, their unreasonable grandfather and boss, had decreed—on Christmas Day no less!—that he wanted Griff O'Hare, the baddest of Celebrity Land's bad boys to provide the entertainment at the ball.

Kinga was not happy with Callum's suggestion, and Tinsley didn't blame her. She had no idea how her sister was going to resolve that thorny problem but had no doubt she would.

They were both very experienced at pulling last minute rabbits out of top hats.

The DJ cranked up the volume, another bartender joined the attractive staff at the bar and alcohol flowed like water. Tinsley sensed that she wasn't going to get to bed before dawn and the thought made her want to cry. She'd worked eighteen-hour days for three days straight and she was exhausted. She wanted her bed, to cuddle Moose, her enormous Maine Coon cat, to spend New Year's Day with her just-older sister, Kinga, and Jules, her best friend.

Tinsley straightened her shoulders and rolled her head from side to side, trying to ease the stiffness in her muscles. She needed a double shot of caffeine, or an energy drink, and she would be fine. Okay, maybe not *fine* but she would cope. Coping was what she did.

She refused to let people see her looking anything other than happy and content. She might be paddling like crazy under the surface, but she was damned if she'd let anyone see her sweat. Even when her husband bailed after twelve years together and their divorce rocked the foundations of her world, nobody except for Kinga had seen Tinsley cry.

No, she was a Ryder-White and they did not wear their hearts on their sleeves. She would rather be thought of as cold and unfeeling than pitiful and weak.

Tinsley felt movement behind her and turned,

holding back her sigh. She didn't feel like dealing with Cody Gallant right now...

Truthfully, she never felt like dealing with Cody.

Cody held two champagne glasses in one big hand and a bottle of Moët in the other. After pouring the pale gold liquid into the glasses, and handing one to her, he placed the bottle on the high table between them. Echoing her earlier stance, he rested his forearms on the railing, his gaze moving from the action on the dance floor below to the VIP area across from them. She had seen Cody in that area earlier, chatting with the men and charming the women, utterly at ease with Toronto's elite. She wasn't surprised; Cody could talk to princes and peasants, celebrities and custodians. As the owner and operator of a company specializing in staging spectacular events, from music festivals to sports races to high-society weddings, he knew how to work a room. The Gallant and the Ryder families ran in the same Portland, Maine, circles but even with a pedigree, one had to be at the top of their game to secure Ryder International's business. Cody did that in spades.

Tinsley didn't understand why he'd chosen to grace this event with his presence. She knew his company was staging massive New Year's Eve parties in both Los Angeles and New York tonight. He should be there, at either of those events, so his appearance here hours earlier had surprised the hell out of her.

Tinsley refused to ask for an explanation. She

tried not to speak to Cody more than was necessary. She sipped champagne, thinking of the differences between her ex-husband and his brother. Cody was four years older than JT and different in looks and personality. Whereas JT was blond and thin, Cody topped out at six-three or -four, and under his tailored designer tuxedo was a hard and muscled body.

With his rugged, masculine looks—square jaw, long nose and quick-to-smile eyes and mouth—Cody looked like he could grace the cover of any men's fitness magazine. JT had been a hipster before hipsters were fashionable—wearing a beard and his blond shoulder-length hair pulled back into a stubby tail. Cody kept his wavy, dark-as-midnight hair short. The brothers shared the same eyes, a deep green shade that reminded Tinsley of freshly cut Christmas trees. She could always read JT's eyes, but Cody kept all his emotions behind a green velvet curtain.

It was commonly accepted that Cody was bigger, hotter, so much sexier than his younger brother. JT was bookish, nerdy, intense…and, when people compared him to Cody, they seemed to imply that JT was a faded version of his brother.

It was a truth she could now admit and yet another bullet point on her list of things that annoyed her about Cody. Others were that he'd never tried to get to know her and that he kept his distance from her. And when he did talk to her, he was terse, sometimes borderline rude. She'd never been the recipient of his famous charm. Not that she wanted to be but...*whatever.*

Tinsley released a breath, reminding herself that her biggest gripe with Cody was that he'd never approved of her and JT's relationship. He'd even, the night before their wedding—the one she'd planned with exquisite attention paid to every detail—begged her not to go through with the ceremony. It wouldn't last, he told her. He had been proved right and Tinsley hated that he'd predicted their future.

She still desperately wanted to know what he'd realized back then that she hadn't, but her pride refused to allow her to utter the words.

And what did it matter? She and JT were divorced, and he had a new wife and a new life. She had her job at Ryder International.

"Why are you here, overseeing this event?" she demanded.

Cody turned his eyes on her; they were the most amazing color and they always made her feel a little off-balance and jumpy.

"What do you mean?"

"I know you have events happening tonight, one in LA and another in New York."

"And one in New Orleans, too."

That wasn't any type of an answer. Tinsley released an irritated sigh. "Surely those events should be higher on your list of priorities."

Cody stared down at the dance floor, his broad back hunched. "I decide my priorities, no one else.

And I employ good people who can handle the events."

"You didn't answer my question,"

He turned his head to look at her and Tinsley felt like a bug under a microscope. She had known him since she was fifteen years old and, although almost another fifteen plus years had passed, she still felt like a gawky teenager. Something about him made her feel edgy.

"Ryder International was my first client and there would be no Gallant Events without the chance your grandfather gave me. I will always look after Ryder International business personally," Cody replied.

Tinsley released an annoyed sigh, reluctantly impressed by his statement. Cody was one of the few people who got along well with her crabby grandfather, and he was someone Callum could tolerate for more than a half hour.

Callum Ryder-White was exceptionally difficult, but he was also the most talented businessman of his generation. When he took control of the family-owned chain of bars, with help from his younger brother, Benjamin, the company was facing insolvency. The brothers turned the business around. After Ben's premature death, Callum flew higher, achieving heights his father and grandfather had only dreamed of. Now, after forty-five years at the helm, Callum was in control of a ten-billion-dollar chain of luxury bars situated in fifty luxury hotels in twenty countries. Callum might be a brilliant businessman, but he lacked people skills, and his family and staff, for the most part, annoyed him. He was a hard-driving, cold leader who pushed his family to be the very best—and then constantly undermined their talent.

The same couldn't be said of Cody Gallant. Tinsley had worked with many of his employees and she had yet to hear a bad word spoken about him. He was, reputedly, fair and supportive. He paid well and treated his staff with respect. He and Callum were very different, but they still got along, possibly because Cody had never been afraid to stand up to the old man.

Callum also respected Cody's ambition and his drive, often saying that few people could match Ryder International's meteoric rise, but Cody came close. Gallant Events had branches all over the country and Cody had satellite offices in London, Tokyo and Sydney. Callum liked taking credit for being the first to recognize Cody's talent.

Callum liked taking credit, period.

Cody stood up straight and gestured to the masses below. "Would you like to?"

"Would I like to what?" Tinsley asked, confused.

"Dance."

"With you?" She and Cody didn't dance—God, they barely *spoke*.

"No one else around so, yes, with me."

"Why would you ask me that?" Tinsley demanded, pushing away the thought of what it would be like to be plastered against that hard chest as they swayed to a slow song.

"I like to dance and it's New Year's Eve," Cody responded, his mouth lifting in his world-famous half smile, half smirk. It was, Tinsley reluctantly admitted, as sexy as hell.

"I saw you in the VIP area earlier, and there were at least five women who passed you their phone numbers. I'm fairly sure any of them would accept your invitation to dance," Tinsley replied. "I'm working."

He didn't respond but he kept his eyes on her, intense but also a little amused.

"Besides, I don't dance," Tinsley reluctantly told him.

"Everybody dances." Cody shrugged. He downed his glass of champagne and poured another.

Everyone but her. She was rhythm and music impaired. A flaw she'd never managed to overcome.

"Not me. It's not in my skill set."

"You can't be that bad," Cody insisted. "Surely even you can shuffle your feet and bob your head."

She probably could, but she'd seen Cody dance at various functions over the years. He was one of those annoying men who had rhythm, someone who was naturally graceful. First on the dance floor, the last to leave it.

No, dancing with Gallant was out of the question. Tinsley sighed, wishing she could move her body with confidence, feel the music deep inside and let go. But that wasn't who she was. She kept a tight lid on her wilder impulses. She was a rational, thoughtful and logical person, and there wasn't much space in her life for the uncontrollable, for coloring outside the lines. She believed in structure, in schedules, and hated surprises or situations where she felt out of control. Or foolish.

Dancing made her feel very foolish indeed.

"No, thank you."

"I will get you to dance," Cody softly told her, his voice just discernible over the pounding music. "Hopefully, sooner than later."

Tinsley handed him a cool smile and deliberately glanced at her watch. "It's nearly time to bring out the midnight buffet. I'm going to check on that." She nodded to the VIP area, where two scantily dressed women wearing very low-cut dresses were hanging over the railing, desperate to get Cody's attention. "You'd better go before they fall off the balcony and into the crowd."

"They aren't nearly as interesting as you," Tinsley thought she heard Cody say as she walked away. But that couldn't be right. She and Cody didn't like each other. They'd been enemies for years and had they not been business associates and connected through their families, they'd avoid each other.

They had, as it was said, irreconcilable differences.

When Tinsley disappeared from view, Cody turned his back to the VIP area and ran his hands over his face.

So, that went well.

He'd decided, a few days ago, that if he was going to make a New Year's resolution—something he wasn't in the habit of doing—it would be to improve his relationship with Tinsley Ryder-White.

It might be a fool's errand. But after fifteen years of snapping and snarling at each other, it was time to get over themselves. She'd married and divorced his all-but-estranged brother and it was time they moved the hell on. They weren't kids anymore, for God's sake.

Cody could remember the first time he saw Tinsley, later to be known, along with her sister, Kinga, as Portland's Princesses. It was summer and he'd dragged JT away from his computer to join him and some friends for a day on the beach. He'd been worried about his younger brother and thought he needed to get out more. Cody accepted that JT wasn't a people person like him, but social interaction was important. As was getting the occasional dose of vitamin D. And breathing fresh air.

Cody had been walking out of the surf when he saw Tinsley approaching JT, who sat on a towel, looking miserable. She wore a conservative black one-piece bathing suit under a pair of denim shorts and her dark hair, a couple of shades lighter than his, was pulled off her heart-shaped face into a high tail that bobbed when she walked. She was young—too young for him—but she was gorgeous. Pale skin, pronounced cheekbones and a mouth made to sin. At twenty-one, he'd liked to sin...

He'd watched as Tinsley stopped in front of JT and spoke to him. It took JT a moment to respond and then, to Cody's amazement, his shy brother patted his towel and invited her to sit down. Cody stared at them, blond and dark, and felt despair swamp him.

She wouldn't be good for JT. He wouldn't be good for her. They'd eventually hurt each other.

It was a snap judgment, and he'd had no evidence to support his feelings, but he'd known it like he knew his name. He'd been proved right.

Cody shook off the memories. That was in the past. She and JT had been divorced for a while now, and his brother lived on the other side of the world. Cody's oldest and classiest client was Ryder International and, while his contracts with them weren't his biggest or the most lucrative, being associated with the famous brand was a shining star on his corporate résumé.

Tinsley co-led the publicity department with her sister, and with this year being Ryder's centennial year, they were planning some kick-ass events that would garner massive attention. He'd conducted a series of meetings with Callum and was expecting contracts to organize various events both in the States and overseas.

The events wouldn't be piddly opening nights, but multimillion-dollar projects that would garner international attention. That his company was well respected and enormously lucrative was in no doubt. But organizing the Ryder centennial events would make Gallant Events the go-to company for rich, exciting clients from every corner of the world, and he'd be right up there with the best of the best.

Exactly where he'd always aimed to be.

But to get there, he would have to personally oversee the initial stages of every project. If he was going to sink or swim—and he very much intended to swim—it would be by his efforts, not by anyone else's.

He'd have to work closely with both of Portland's Princesses. He and Kinga got along, but Tinsley was his brother's ex. JT had left for Hong Kong with no warning and a few days later, Tinsley received a call telling her he wasn't returning and that he'd filed for divorce. Cody still wanted to rearrange JT's face for blindsiding her and for being such a selfish prick.

He thought he'd raised his brother better than that.

But JT hadn't given Tinsley, her feelings or his marriage another thought. Cody even flew to Hong Kong to talk some sense into his brother, but it was obvious that JT had moved on and that he no longer wanted to be with Tinsley.

JT said he wasn't interested in lectures and that he was a grown man and didn't need Cody telling him what to do anymore, or how to do it.

They hadn't spoken since.

Cody sighed, remembering their tense discussion and his inability to reach his brother. To him, marriage meant family and family equaled obligation and responsibility. After his mom's death the year he turned twelve, his father told him it was his duty to look after his younger brother. So Cody listened and did what he was told. It took him a long time to realize his father hadn't wanted to be inconvenienced by his sons so he'd passed the parenting buck to his oldest child.

Cody'd been the one to raise JT. He'd bought him clothes, made sure he did his homework, that he was eating right and wasn't being bullied because of his big brain. Thanks to his father's selfishness and emotional distance, he'd been an adult long before his time.

And, yeah, because he'd spent his teens and early twenties looking after his brother, he'd vowed he'd never again allow himself to feel trapped. A permanent lover—a girlfriend or a wife—was just another person to feel responsible for. Emotions were pointless and only got in the way. So he limited himself to one-night stands and quick flings.

Marriage was completely out of the question and definitively not for him.

Cody allowed his gaze to drift over the room, satisfied that everything was as it should be. Waiters were starting to set up the late-evening buffet in the far corner behind the bar and guests were already lining up to fill their plates. He lifted his eyes to the VIP area and the blonde from earlier who still had her eyes on him. He knew that if he wanted it he'd have company for the rest of the night.

He wasn't even tempted. When he compared her

to Tinsley, she came up short. She was too over-the-top and in your face. Unlike Tinsley's classy gown, the hem of her dress was about six inches too short, her top far too low. She was trying too hard...

Tinsley didn't try at all.

Cody shook his head, wondering what the hell was wrong with him. He was a guy and normally never objected to short skirts and low tops. In fact, he appreciated them. And why was he comparing Fun Girl to Portland's prissiest princess? The one didn't have anything to do with the other.

Despite having known Tinsley for half of her life, she was only a work colleague and he intended to keep it that way.

Princesses were a pain in the ass.

Two

Tinsley left the bar and pulled a scarf from the inside pocket of her calf-length coat and wrapped it around her neck.

It was four in the morning and freezing. She had a short walk back to her hotel and when she got there, she intended to take a scalding-hot shower, pull on her most comfortable pj's and order a cup of hot chocolate from room service. Then she planned to sleep until noon. Her flight back to Portland was in the afternoon, so she'd pass the time by sleeping until the last possible moment.

It had been a long week.

"Tinsley!"

She turned at the deep voice and saw Cody hurrying toward her, his hands buried deep in the pockets of his tan cashmere coat. A light dusting of snow covered his hair and she wondered if he had been waiting for her.

"I'll walk you to your hotel," he told her.

She started to tell him that she was perfectly able to manage the short walk herself, that she'd been navigating her way home alone for a long, long time but the words wouldn't come. Mostly because she'd run out of energy. She shrugged. If he wanted to tromp around in the snow, that was his prerogative.

Tinsley resumed walking and licked a snowflake off her top lip, thinking how beautiful the night was. Portland got its fair share of snow, probably more than most, but she loved winter. She liked moments like this when it was so quiet, when the snow softened the buildings and sidewalks. Despite Cody's presence, it was magical, picture-perfect.

Cody stopped and pulled his phone out of the inside pocket of his tuxedo jacket. Tinsley wondered whom he would be calling so late at night—correction, so early in the morning. Instead of lifting the device to his ear, he stabbed the screen with his index finger. A few moments later, a mournful voice, singing in French, pierced the quiet night.

"Edith Piaf," Cody told her with a small smile on his handsome face. "Everybody needs to dance to Edith on a cold, snowy night once in their lives."

Was he mad? It was cold, her feet were aching, she was exhausted and he wanted to dance?

He was insane; that was the only explanation.

"Cody, I don't dance," was all she could think to say. But suddenly she was no longer quite as tired, and, strangely, her feet had stopped throbbing.

Cody held out his hand, his expression daring her to join him. "I do," he told her as her hand slid into his. With his free hand, he unbuttoned her coat and slid his hand over her hip. The thin material of her dress was no barrier to the heat of his palm and she shuddered, wondering why she felt like she had been plugged into a wall socket. Or heated from the inside out.

This was Cody, not someone she was supposed to react to. He was her ex-brother-in-law.

The last person in the world who should be making her feel…hot, alive, bubbling with anticipation.

She'd been in an emotional and physical cocoon since her divorce and JT was the last man she'd kissed, made love with. Now she was wondering whether Cody's lips were as soft as they looked, how he tasted.

God, she wanted to kiss Cody.

She really, *really* wanted to kiss him. What on earth was happening to her?

Before she could find an answer to that question, Cody's big hand on her back pulled her to him, his other clasping her right hand. "Do what I do," he murmured, his breath warm against her ear.

She tried to follow along; she did, but her coordination, already bad at the best of times, was ham-

pered by the pounding in her ears, the prickling of
her skin. He was a lot taller than her and despite her
heels, the top of her head only brushed his chin. If
she tipped her head back, she could look into his
eyes...

She was not going to tip her head back.

Tinsley stepped on his shoe and she heard his
swift intake of breath. Cody released a small laugh.
"Wow, you *are* bad at this," he said, sounding
amused.

"Told you," Tinsley replied, releasing a long sigh.

He stopped trying to shuffle her around and
looked down at her face, his eyes a deep, dangerous
green in the golden glow of the streetlight. Tinsley
couldn't take her eyes off him, fascinated by the intensity in his gaze, the way his fingers pushed into
her lower back, his touch turning possessive. He was
just holding her, but her panties turned damp and her
need for pressure and friction increased.

If he didn't kiss her soon, touch her with more
than a hand on her lower back, she might just scream.
Not recognizing herself, Tinsley curled her hand
around the back of his neck, and standing on her
tiptoes, pulled his head down and slammed her lips
against his. He didn't react and Tinley tensed.

She'd only ever known one other man and it
had been a long time and she could be reading him
wrong...

She was about to pull back when Cody's lips
started to nibble hers, light, lovely kisses that fanned

the raging fire in her belly, deep in her womb. But light and lovely wasn't what she needed or wanted.

She wanted to step inside the fire and burn...

Increasing the pressure on the back of his neck, she opened her mouth and her tongue darted out and slipped past his teeth. She felt him tense and thought he was about to pull back. *Please don't*, Tinsley silently begged him.

Another few seconds passed, and just when she thought this was a lost cause, Cody gently gripped her jaw and chin and tipped her face to the side and proceeded to kiss her senseless. There was no other word for it; his mouth ravaged hers, hot and hard and insistent. His other hand slid between her dress and coat and skimmed down her hip, around to her butt, pulling her closer, so close that she could feel his hard erection pushing into her stomach. Yum.

Desperate, Tinsley slid her hand between them to open the single coat button, hurriedly pushing aside his tuxedo jacket to get as close to him as she could. Through his thin dress shirt, she could feel hot skin and hard muscles and, not recognizing herself, she yanked his shirt out from his pants, pulling it up so she could lay her hands on his warm, wonderful masculine skin.

She'd missed this, missed the feel of muscles under her hands, the slightly rough texture of a man's skin. She'd missed feeling feminine and powerful and desired and sexy...

And she wanted more. She wanted them naked,

him inside her, driving into her as they spun toward that fireball of intense pleasure. No, it was more than want—she *needed* him. She needed everything he could give her.

Not allowing herself to think this through, or talk herself out of this once-in-a-blue-moon madness, she pulled her mouth off Cody's and stared into his beautiful, oh-so-masculine face. "Stay with me tonight—sleep with me."

"That's the last thing I expected you to say."

She didn't blame him for saying that, acting impulsively wasn't what she did, who she was. She shrugged and tried to smile. "It's that magical hour when time and reality are suspended."

His fingers were still on her jaw and she saw the hesitation in his eyes. She shook her head and knew that if he spoke, he'd turn her down. That wasn't an option.

"One night, tonight. Let's pretend we're strangers, that we've never met before, that we saw each other in the club and started to dance. It's the New Year and we're looking to see it in with a bang," she said, hoping he didn't notice the hint of desperation in her voice, "figuratively and literally."

A small smile touched Cody's mouth but didn't reach his eyes. "Are you sure about this, Tinsley? Once we do this, we can't go back."

"When dawn breaks this will all be a dream," Tinsley told him. "And everything will be as it was before."

"You're naive if you think that," Cody told her, his voice rough.

"I want you, Cody. I want sex, a physical connection," Tinsley insisted. "One night of pleasure, no expectations, and no demands. That's what you do, isn't it?"

Annoyance flashed in his eyes, but she didn't care. All she wanted was his word that, when they reached her hotel, he'd remind her of how it felt to be held, desired…*wanted*. It had been too long… way too long.

"Are you sure about this, Tinsley?" Cody demanded.

No, not at all.

But she was going to do it anyway.

Cody knew that sleeping with Tinsley was a bad idea, that he was making a big-ass mistake, but his body wasn't listening to his brain. Tinsley Ryder-White, so lovely, wanted to get lucky and she wanted to get lucky with *him*.

He'd have to be a fool or a saint to say no. He was neither.

But, he told himself, as she opened the door to her hotel room, he wasn't allowed to complain when this came back to bite him on the ass. And it would. She thought they were going to be able to have one night of bed-banging sex and then not see each other for a few weeks, possibly a month or two. She didn't know that Callum had implied there was a lot of Ryder International work coming Cody's way…

Before he saw her naked, she should know that.

The door slammed behind him and he watched Tinsley drop her coat to the floor and step out of her heels. She lifted her hands to her hair and yanked out a series of bobby pins and her long, wavy hair tumbled down her back. She tossed the pins in the direction of the credenza and stood before him in her silver, calf-length cocktail dress, looking like a dressed-up, sexy fairy.

Sweet, sexy, a little wild…

He swallowed, looking for moisture to coat his mouth. He needed to speak, before this went any further. "Tinsley, we need to talk."

His words died as her fingers went to the zip under her left armpit and he watched, mesmerized as the fabric parted to show a slash of pale, creamy flesh and a small breast.

"I don't want to talk, Cody," Tinsley told him, her voice oh-so-serious. "I want to kiss, and touch and taste, but I most definitely *don't* want to talk."

"But—"

Jesus, he was about to swallow his tongue. Her dress fell to her hips, revealing her breasts, tipped with small, coral-colored nipples. They were already puckered—from the cold or from her being aroused—and he couldn't wait to pull them into his mouth, to taste their sweetness.

"Tonight you're not someone I've known for half of my life, you are not my ex-brother-in-law, you're just a guy I picked up in a bar, okay?"

There was so much wrong with that sentence, but

Cody couldn't make sense of any of it because his head was swimming and his cock was jumping and *he wanted her more than he'd ever wanted anyone before.* He sucked in a breath of much-needed air, thinking that he owed it to her to tell her that this might be a mistake. He shook his head, trying to say the right words, to get his point across. But, before he could, Tinsley shimmied the dress over her hips and placed a hand on her hip, all long limbs, black hair and passion in her deep, dark eyes.

How was he supposed to think, and talk, when all she wore was a tiny triangle of nude-colored lace, frothy and insubstantial?

God, he loved women's underwear.

"Are you just going to stand there?" Tinsley demanded, stepping forward to push his coat off his shoulders.

He was lost, his concerns and worries melting like early-morning mist on a hot summer's day. Cody swiped his mouth across hers, then kissed her jaw, her throat, slowly moving down to her lovely breasts. He dragged his tongue over her nipple, and it tasted sweeter than he imagined. Her sigh, followed by a breathy groan, told him she was eager for more.

He'd tried to talk to her but she only had one thing on her mind. Him.

And he was very okay with that.

So far, the morning after was living up to its reputation of being super awkward, Tinsley thought, lifting her eyes to the mirror above the sink. Her hair was a cloud of tangled curls, her mascara had left her eyelashes and had formed two dark streaks under her red-rimmed-from-no-sleep eyes and her mouth tasted like a crime scene. She wore Cody's shirt—now missing two buttons from where she'd ripped it open last night in her haste to get to his skin—and she had beard rash on her jaw. And on her breasts. And between her legs.

Tinsley gripped the basin and, unable to look at her reflection anymore, straightened her arms and dropped her head to look at the tiled floor. Last night, swept away by lust, she hadn't thought about how to deal with the morning after. Frankly, from the moment she and Cody first kissed, she hadn't thought beyond them getting naked.

But here she was, hiding out in the bathroom, wishing he'd leave.

Tinsley knew that, in theory, she was making a mountain out of a pile of rocks. He'd wanted sex, she'd wanted sex and so they'd had sex. Amazing, no-commitment sex. They'd woken up tangled in each other's arms and indulged in sleepy, best-way-to-wake-up, one-last-time-before-we-move-on sex.

It was now time to wash her face, brush her teeth and usher him out the door, hoping like hell they could avoid each other until the memory of this night faded. How long would that take? A few weeks? A couple of months? But, since it was the best sex she'd had in her life, she doubted she'd ever forget the hours she spent in Cody's arms…

Dammit.

From the moment she dropped her dress, clothes started flying, both of them desperate to be skin on skin, to discover each other's heat. They were on fire for each other, they *were* fire, both wanting to scorch and be scorched.

Surprisingly, and a little irritatingly, Cody knew how to touch her, how to make her moan and groan, to writhe and to want. He kissed and sucked her nipples, his fingers and tongue between her legs were achingly familiar, his mutters of appreciation the sweetest music she'd ever heard. Tinsley had to remind herself that this was Cody, the man with whom she'd always had a tense relationship.

And when he nudged her legs open with his knee, held her hips in his broad hands to slide into her with one smooth stroke, she felt complete, like he was the missing piece of a puzzle she didn't know was unfinished. And when he came, she relished the sounds he made—appreciative and awestruck, powerful and just a little vulnerable.

His big body collapsed on hers and she could still feel his weight pushing her into the soft mattress, his thick wavy hair between her fingers, the intoxicating smell of sex and satisfaction. After round one, they'd dozed, her head on his chest, her hand on his muscled stomach, his hand on her bare butt. And she'd felt safe, protected, a little cherished. As they drifted in and out of sleep, if she moved, he followed, tightening his hold, putting his leg across her and tangling them up tighter. And, inevitably, their sleepy caresses turned deeper and darker, more demanding.

They made love three times last night and once this morning, each time as good as the first. She hadn't wanted to stop touching him, breathing him in, touching his strong, big, powerful body.

And because the beauty of their amazing, unexpected connection threatened to overwhelm her, she'd wrenched herself out of his arms, yanked on his shirt and stumbled to the bathroom, knowing that if she didn't pull away, she'd ask him to stay.

And stay. And stay...

But this was *Cody*, she reminded herself, her ex-brother-in-law. She wasn't supposed to be feeling this way, liking him—no, loving sex—this much. She had to be reacting this way because he was her first one-night stand, her first experience of no-commitment sex, and she was making this into something so much more than what it was...

It was hot sex, nothing more, nothing less. In a few hours, the hormones careering around her body would wear off, the effects of dopamine would fade and she'd be the logical, rational person she always was. She just needed time and distance...

This was lust, and it would dwindle to nothing.

Tinsley pushed her hands into her hair, finger-combed her tangles and washed off her makeup. She brushed her teeth and, feeling a little more human, walked back into the room to see Cody pulling on his pants, his broad chest still bare. He had a light smattering of dark hair on his chest and the most gorgeous happy trail...one she'd followed with her tongue.

Stop that, Tinsley. It's over. Done. Time to move on...

"I ordered coffee," Cody told her.

Tinsley nodded her thanks and walked over to the bed and sat on the edge, looking down at the bedside cabinet, to where their identical phones lay. She wished she could find something witty and breezy to say, something that would cut through the tension. She couldn't think of anything...

"Are you okay?" Cody asked her, sitting down next to her to pull on his socks.

"Sure," Tinsley replied, knowing that even if she wasn't, she'd never admit to being anything other than okay. She was stubborn that way; the more uncomfortable or out of her depth she felt, the more confident and calm she appeared.

As Cody walked to the bathroom and pulled the door shut behind him, her phone buzzed. She picked it up, swiped her finger over the screen and saw the text message appear.

Can't wait to see you at Luca's tonight, it's been ages since we saw each other. Maybe we can have our own New Year's Eve celebration.

Wink, wink...

Norah? The only Norah she knew was a designer and decorator she and Kinga occasionally hired to stage some of their functions. She was well regarded as being one of the best in the business, but they weren't social friends and hadn't made any plans for tonight.

Tinsley pushed the home screen button and saw the higgledy-piggledy mess on the screen. This was Cody's phone, not hers. And, judging by this text message, he and Norah were more than work friends.

Cody and the gorgeous Norah made sense. Norah was loud, confident and was one of those women who oozed sexuality. Norah, Tinsley was sure, would know what she was doing in the bedroom…

Tinsley had just followed Cody's lead. Should she have been more aggressive, more demanding? Had she been too passive, too acquiescent? Was he disappointed in her? Did he think she'd wasted his time?

Suddenly what they'd shared, what had been beautiful a few hours ago, seemed tawdry, a little tasteless.

And, yeah, she didn't like feeling ick after sex.

God, this would be her first and last one-night stand. She simply wasn't cut out for them.

But she'd never let him know that. No, she'd smile, hand him his phone and find a way to ease out of this situation with as much grace as she could muster. She'd never let him see her sweat…

When he returned to stand in front of her, she nodded to his phone. "A message came through and

I read it. Sorry, I thought it was mine. The phones look identical…"

An emotion she couldn't identify flashed in his eyes as he took the phone, read the message and tossed the phone on the bed without replying or giving her an explanation…

Not that she was owed one.

Tinsley slid her hands under her thighs and pulled a cool smile onto her face. "Last night, thank you." She forced herself to pick up his wrist to look at his expensive watch. "I'm going to shower and then I'm going to go back to sleep for a few hours."

Cody frowned, looking like he wanted to argue with her. She spoke again, her words rushed. "I'll see you back in the city at some point and, I'm pretty sure about this, we'll be irritating each other before long. It is, after all, what we do best."

Cody glanced at the bed, his look suggesting that they'd found something they were much better at than annoying each other. She wasn't going to acknowledge his unspoken words so instead sent him a cool smile. "Have a good trip home, Cody. Lock the door on the way out, won't you?"

She walked away from him, her head held high and her back straight. She made it to the door to the bathroom before her name on his lips halted her progress. Turning, she lifted her eyebrows.

He gestured to her torso and the corners of his mouth pulled up into a sexy-as-hell smirk. "I need my shirt and you're wearing it."

Tinsley looked down and nodded. Right. The cuffs hung over her hands and the tails almost reached her knees. It was soft and smelled of his sexy cologne. She didn't want to give it up…

"God, you are so sexy standing there in my shirt," Cody said, his voice rough with desire. Tinsley met his eyes and desire arced between them, raising the temperature in the room.

He wanted her. Again… And if she gave him the least little bit of encouragement, he'd stay and that bed would see a lot more action.

She wanted to kiss that strong jaw again, bite the cords of his neck, run her tongue over the muscles in his arms, across his ladderlike stomach…

It would be so easy…

Her eyes bounced to his phone on his bed and she remembered Norah, and that she was expecting to see him later. The thought of Cody jumping from her bed to another woman's caused nausea to swirl in her stomach.

Yeah, she definitely wasn't any good at one-night stands…

Feeling reckless, irrationally pissed off and very off-balance, Tinsley crossed her arms over her body and gripped the hem of his shirt and slowly, oh so slowly, pulled it up, revealing her naked body inch by inch. Even though he was across the room, she heard the swift intake of his breath, and when she looked into his eyes, they were deep and dark and full of passion.

It was obvious what he wanted…and damn her for wanting it too.

But the moment was gone; it was time to move on. He had, after all, other fish to fry.

She pulled his shirt over her head, scrunched it into a ball and threw it. Without another word, she stepped into the bathroom and slammed the door shut.

And, because she didn't trust herself, she locked it.

Three

Knowing his father was out for the morning, James walked down the long corridor to Callum's corner office suite to talk to his father's longtime personal assistant. She was also the woman with whom he had an on-off affair from the time he was eighteen to twenty-three.

It wasn't something they ever acknowledged.

James rubbed the back of his neck, unable to remember how the affair started or who made the first move: the cocky, spoiled teenager, or the then thirty-year-old Emma? During the summer before he left for college, he'd fallen deeply, crazily in love with her.

Despite their age difference, their secret affair lasted all through his college career. Emma repeatedly told him they didn't have a future together— his father had other plans for him— and James countered her pessimism by violently insisting he'd defy his father to keep her in his life. Firmly believing he'd had the upper hand—so cocky, so spoiled— he'd issued an ultimatum. They stopped sneaking around and came clean or he'd call it quits, over forever.

Emma called his bluff and shattered his heart.

In pain, and because he'd inherited his father's stupid pride, he'd immediately flung himself back into the rarefied society of the rich East Coast and met Penelope, young, pretty and eminently suitable. Within a month of meeting her, and with Callum's blessing, he'd asked her to marry him, and within three they were legally hitched and stitched.

And when he returned from his honeymoon, he realized Emma was pregnant and that her child was his.

Emma refused to confirm or deny his allegations, she simply shut down every non-work-related conversation. She also told him that if he didn't drop the subject, she'd accuse him of sexual harassment. James, not recognizing his ex-lover, and scared about the possible repercussions, backed way off.

Defeated, he set up a trust fund for her child, tried to save his rocky marriage and forget he had a son. Life became easier when Kinga and then Tinsley arrived and he could be the dad he so wanted to be.

Emma finally lifted her eyes to acknowledge his presence.

"Let's imagine I, unknowingly, fathered a child…" James said, standing behind her visitor's chair.

Emma, as he expected, started to stand. James narrowed his eyes and shook his head. "This is important, Emma, I suggest you listen. Sit down."

Emma sank back into her chair, her eyes apprehensive. But she did lift her chin and James took that as a sign to continue.

"Let's also imagine that child was raised by his single mom and was never told who his father is…"

Emma leaned forward and rested her forearms on her desk, her worried eyes not leaving his face.

"That hypothetical child might be interested in his ancestry, whether he had any relations on his father's side that he's never met, or heard of," James said, pacing the area in front of her desk. "He might have registered on the very popular WhoAreYou dot com, hoping to explore those connections."

James pushed his hand into his hair. "Once my DNA is entered into the ancestry website's database, connections will be made. The website will flag a genetic relationship between me and that child, between him and Callum."

Emma's eyes widened as she processed the implications of his pronouncement. James waited for her to speak, hoping she'd, finally, give him a confirmation of his suspicions. But she didn't speak and a pale face and worried eyes did not a confession make.

"Why are you telling me this?" Emma demanded after a tense silence.

"Because the tests results might set off a chain of events for which there will be consequences," James explained.

"Consequences for who? For you and your wife?" Emma demanded.

"For all of us," James replied, shrugging. "I just want all of us to be prepared."

And maybe he also thought she'd finally come clean and admit he was Garrett's father. But no, Emma was still an unbreakable vault.

Emma stared off into space for a few minutes before standing up and crossing her arms over her chest. "All very interesting, James, but I have work to do."

Her expression turned cooler, if that was at all possible, and James sighed. It was Emma speak for "I'm done with discussing this."

Yep, situation normal.

She could ignore him but if Garrett was registered on the DNA site and connections were made, the status quo would seriously upend his life, his marriage and his position within Ryder International. Life, as he knew it, would be over.

Don't-rock-the-boat-James found that scenario appalling, I-want-to-acknowledge-my-son James hoped everything would come out into the open. Either way this dysfunctional cookie crumbled, he'd be disappointed.

Situation normal.

* * *

Neither of them could spare the time to meet with their grandfather, but Callum was the owner of the company and their boss and when he said jump, they jumped. They knew not to rock the boat.

Tinsley parked her butt on the edge of the conference table next to Kinga and stretched out her legs. The conference room had floor-to-ceiling windows looking out onto the harbor downtown and it was, yet again, snowing.

Tinsley remembered tasting snowflakes on her lips just before Cody kissed her, the way he heated her from the inside out. Frankly, she was surprised that during their lovemaking the bed hadn't burst into flames.

It had been the best sex of her life—hot, raunchy and oh so uninhibited. Maybe she had allowed herself to let go because she knew there would be no consequences. After all, Cody wasn't part of her day-to-day life.

She hadn't heard from him, nor seen him, since that night and that worked for her. She could pretend he was a stranger. In her head, she'd had fun sex—numerous times!—with a stranger and not with her ex-brother-in-law.

Kinga nudged her legs with her knee. "Earth to Tinsley."

Tinsley blinked before her eyes focused on her sister's lovely face. Kinga wore her blond hair cut supershort, and a pair of black-framed glasses covered her whiskey-colored eyes.

"Sorry, I was miles away," Tinsley told her.

"You've been very distracted lately," Kinga commented, leaning back in a chair and crossing her legs. "Is everything okay?"

She and Kinga were exceptionally close, something they hadn't been while she'd been with JT. During their courtship and marriage, JT came first and juggling him and her professional life had taken all the time and energy Tinsley had. After their divorce, Kinga was there for her and their friendship was now deep and strong.

But as much as she trusted Kinga, Tinsley wasn't ready to tell her, or anyone, that she and Cody had bumped boots on New Year's Eve. Since they were barely able to conduct a reasonable conversation without sniping at each other, explaining they'd had earth-shattering sex would raise questions she didn't know how to answer.

If Kinga pushed and Tinsley told her sister how she'd spent her last night in Toronto, she'd justify it by saying that it was a little end-of-year madness. She'd remind her that Cody wasn't her type, that he was too alpha, too domineering, blunt and direct. And that they'd kill each other if they spent too much time together…

"Why does Callum want this meeting?" Tinsley asked, changing the subject.

Kinga shrugged. "Why does Callum do anything?"

Kinga's question reminded Tinsley of something else she was curious about. Callum had given them—their parents, and her and Kinga—DNA tests for Christmas, hoping to find out more about their Ryder-White ancestry.

Tinsley didn't particularly care where in the world their genes originated but it was vitally important to Callum. Callum was besotted with keeping the Ryder-White bloodline untainted.

"Have those DNA tests come back yet?" she asked.

Kinga wrinkled her nose. "No, and it's driving Callum nuts. The parental unit is also acting a bit squirrelly."

She'd noticed that as well. Her normally easygoing father, who worked as Callum's right-hand person, was irritable. Their mom was distracted and twitchy. "Should we ask them what's going on?"

Kinga raised her eyebrows. "Uh-uh, I'm not that brave," she answered. "Maybe they're just going through another rough patch."

Their parents didn't have what Tinsley would call a warm marriage. They hadn't raised their voices or their hands, there had been no ugliness, but Tinsley never saw much affection between them either. She knew that theirs was, to an extent, an arranged marriage. Her mom's family had business connections with Callum, and around the time Callum decreed it was time for James to marry, Penelope had been there and waiting.

Tinsley loved her dad, but she wished he was a

little more assertive in standing up to Callum. She knew there was a reason for him being obsequious, had heard an explanation, but couldn't remember the details.

They said that a woman either marries a man a lot like her dad, or the exact opposite of him. JT was a lot like James, easygoing, not one to rock the boat, happy to be managed and directed...

Until the day he wasn't.

When she married again, she wouldn't choose someone like her dad...

What the hell was she thinking? She wasn't ever marrying again! She'd placed her love and faith and trust in a man who'd promised to love her until death, yet he hadn't managed to keep that promise beyond her twenty-seventh birthday.

Tinsley knew that after all her work keeping their relationship alive and on track, if she couldn't make it work with JT, there was no chance of her having a successful relationship with anyone else.

There was simply no point in risking her heart again. Being single, she didn't have to worry about anyone else, didn't need to consult or consider anyone else. After twelve years of shepherding JT through life, she felt free.

Kinga's finger drilled into her thigh and pulled Tinsley back into the conversation. "Ow!"

"Expect more of those if you keep drifting off," Kinga told her. "You're not normally so distracted, Tins. What's going on?"

Tinsley sent Kinga an apologetic look. "Sorry. It's been a long year."

"It's the seventh, Tins, of *January*," Kinga retorted. "We're only one week in."

"God," Tinsley groaned.

Not wanting to answer any questions, or even think about Cody Gallant, she changed the subject. "Haven't you just come back from Manhattan?"

"I flew in last night."

"And how did your meeting go with Griff O'Hare?"

Kinga released a small growl. "The man is arrogant, stubborn and far too good looking for his own good!"

Tinsley's eyebrows shot up in surprise. *Wow.* That was quite a reaction from her normally even keeled sister.

Tinsley wanted to know more, but heard footsteps coming down the hallway and she quickly stood up.

As Callum took his place at the head of the table, Tinsley turned her back to the door to walk around the table to take her seat, rolling her eyes at Kinga at Callum's irritable demand for an update on the Valentine's Day ball. Her father took his seat and sent her a wan smile. He looked tired and pale, Tinsley decided, and not at all like her normally happy and hearty father.

Kinga gave Callum her report, making it obvious that she was not happy that Callum had signed Griff O'Hare, the bad boy performer, to sing at the ball, without consulting her. Unlike James, Tinsley and Kinga both argued with their grandfather—not often and only about things that mattered—and the fact that they still had jobs made them think he tolerated their impertinence. Tinsley made notes on her iPad and when she looked up, her eyes widened at the sight of Cody Gallant sliding into a chair opposite her.

Two thoughts jostled for prominence in her brain: he looked scrumptious, dressed in gray suit pants, and a cranberry-colored sweater worn under a smart black jacket. And, secondly, what the hell was he doing here? Dark stubble covered his cheeks and she remembered how that scruff felt between her legs, the gorgeous, sexy itchiness against her sensitive skin. And then he moved his mouth up...

Heat climbed her neck and into her cheeks and she wished the world would open and swallow her whole. She wasn't ready, in any way, shape or form to deal with Cody Gallant. She'd thought she might have some time to perfect her reaction to him but here he was, just a scant week later, sitting opposite her. And all she could do was...blush.

Kinga interrupted her conversation with Callum to lean across the table, her expression concerned. "Are you feeling okay, Tins? You're looking a little flushed."

Cody smirked and Tinsley narrowed her eyes at him. She waved her sister's words away. "I think I'm getting a cold. I'll dose myself with vitamin C and zinc. They say zinc is great for upping one's immunity."

Oh, God. Now she was babbling. Tinsley wanted to bang her forehead on the conference table. She was such an idiot! Luckily her phone pinged with a message and while Callum hated being interrupted by cell phones, she picked it up and waved it. "Sorry, I need to get this."

Because if she ducked her head to stare at the screen, her hair would hide her flaming cheeks. She swiped her thumb across the screen and saw Cody's name.

Need help getting out of that hole you're digging?

You are such a jerk! was the best reply she could think of.

Tossing her head and placing her phone on the table, Tinsley looked at her grandfather, feeling irritated and off-balance.

"Callum, I have another meeting in ten minutes—" she didn't but she had no problem with lying if it would get her out of this room and away from Cody "—so can we move this one along?"

Callum frowned at her impertinence and Tinsley knew he was debating whether to remind her that he was the boss and paid her salary. He didn't need to; Callum frequently repeated those words. Tinsley had, over the years, considered jumping ship and working somewhere else, but working for her grandfather did have its perks: they were paid well above the industry norm and they enjoyed a lot of overseas travel on Callum's private jet.

And let's be honest here, they were allowed to run some kick-ass PR and publicity projects.

And if she left, there was the chance that Callum would punish James for her defection. Callum was not what one could call reasonable.

Callum tapped his index finger on the surface of the sleek black conference table. "Cody, to get you caught up, Ryder International, as part of the centennial celebrations, is sponsoring a horse race in Dubai, a yacht race in Monaco and the Valentine's Day ball is next month."

Tinsley felt compelled to look at Cody and her eyes widened when she noticed he was looking at her. His eyes dropped from her mouth to her chest and when they reconnected with her eyes, she knew where his thoughts were...

They were hanging out with hers in that hotel bedroom, remembering how they almost set the place on fire. Her skin prickled and felt too tight for her body and she couldn't take her eyes off him. She wanted another one-night stand. Hell, she wanted another three or four, ten or twenty.

She simply wanted him.

Their eyes remained connected as Callum's voice faded to a monotonous drawl, and she forgot her father and sister were seated at the table and that she should be paying attention. All she could think of was how Cody's body felt when he settled his hips above hers, that feeling of completeness when he slid inside her, the way the muscle in his jaw contracted, how his breathing grew ragged as he waited for her to come before he did. And how, sometimes, he made her come a few times before following her over the edge...

Kinga, snapping her fingers, pulled Tinsley back to the present moment.

"Sorry, sorry...what did I miss?" Tinsley demanded, wincing when she noticed Callum's furious face. Knowing she needed to do damage control, she rubbed her throat. "Sorry, Callum, I'm not feeling too great. I think I might be getting sick. Would you mind repeating that?"

Callum narrowed his icy blue eyes but before he could speak, Cody jumped in. "Callum wants to add another function to your celebration year," he explained.

What? Was he nuts?

Did Callum have any idea what they were currently dealing with? Kinga—having found out that Callum had already sent the performer, without their knowledge, a contract for him to be the headline act at the ball—had just spent ten minutes trying to persuade Callum to break the contract.

Callum, being Callum, refused.

Kinga needed to organize the ball as well as keep O'Hare on the straight and narrow—his ability to get into trouble was legendary—so that he didn't taint the ball's reputation with his headline catching, bad boy antics. She had her hands full.

As did Tinsley. She had two more bars to open this year as well as overseeing the horse and yacht races. They were already working long hours and the year had barely begun. Kinga bit the corner of her bottom lip, her eyes reflecting Tinsley's anxiety.

"Before I even ask what you want us to do, you need to know that if you add more functions, Callum, we'll need more staff and a bigger budget," Tinsley told him, keeping her voice firm. "Kinga and I are already stretched thin."

Callum nodded and gestured to Cody. "That's why Cody is here. I'm putting Gallant Events on retainer for the next six months and Cody's company will stage the summer promotions."

Promotions, as in plural. "What are you envisioning, Callum?" Tinsley asked, frowning.

"James, explain."

Tinsley turned sideways to look at her dad, her eyebrows raised. Her dad was a creative guy, and she was interested in what he had to say. Before she and Kinga took over and expanded the Ryder International PR division, their department used to fall under her father's control, one of the few responsibilities Callum allowed him.

"Over dinner a few nights ago, I suggested to Callum that we hold a specialty cocktail competition. By my count, we employ over five hundred mixologists and if we add our independent contractors like

Jules—" Tinsley smiled at him mentioning her best friend, Jules, who was one of the best mixologists in the world and did pop-up bars, promotions and events for Ryder International "—then that figure swells to over seven hundred. The bartenders can either enter as a team or on their own, but they have to create four new cocktails inspired by four special moments over the last one hundred years. For instance, the end of the Second World War, landing on the moon, women getting the vote, the fall of the Berlin Wall… You get the idea."

Damn, but that was a spectacular plan. Tinsley felt her mind spinning with additional ideas and when she caught Kinga's eyes, she saw the excitement on her sister's face. *Go, Dad.*

"I'm envisioning a regional contest, then national, then international, with an expert panel of judges," James continued.

"That's a great idea, Dad," Kinga said, sending him a huge smile. "A hell of a lot of work, but a stunning idea. We could get chefs and food critics to judge, and we could get some of our suppliers to sponsor the prize. We could…"

Callum cleared his throat and pointed his index finger at Kinga. "You, young lady, must concentrate on the ball and keeping Griff O'Hare focused." He turned to Tinsley. "This is your project, yours and Cody's. Take the idea, flesh it out, see if it's viable and what budget we'd need. Bring me a detailed proposal in two weeks."

Tinsley scrunched up her nose. She did not want to work with Cody, not now and not in the future. "I can do a feasibility study, Callum, there's no need to involve Cody at this point."

"Cody's company is already on a monthly retainer. He needs to do something to earn the money we pay him," Callum told her, sounding impatient.

Before she could defend Cody—and why did she want to?—Callum signaled the end of the meeting by pushing back his chair. He placed his age-spotted hands on the conference table and told James and Kinga to leave the room. When the door closed behind them, Callum divided his hot glance between Tinsley and Cody.

"You two have always had a contentious relationship," Callum stated, his voice ice-cold, "and I am aware that you try not to work directly with each other."

Okay, where was her crabby grandfather going with this?

"Let me be clear. I do not care that you were once related, nor do I care whether you like each other or not."

Tinsley wanted to look at Cody but pride kept her eyes on Callum's face; she refused to cower under his hard stare. "The two of you working together on this project is nonnegotiable. And if either of you finds that untenable, you will both be fired. I will not play favorites for family."

"Callum—" Tinsley protested.

Callum's expression, if that was at all possible,

hardened further. "Work together or don't work here at all."

"You are being unreasonable," Tinsley protested, standing up so he wasn't looming over them. Cody also climbed to his feet, his face unreadable.

"My company, my rules," Callum stated, straightening. "You have ten days to draw up a feasibility plan and a working budget."

It had been two weeks five minutes ago. "Callum, we need more time."

"We need, at the very least, two months, Callum," Cody told her grandfather. He sent Callum a mocking look. "And if that doesn't suit, feel free to accept my resignation. I think you've forgotten that, while Ryder International was my first client, it most certainly isn't my *only* client. In fact, you're not even in my top ten. Fire me—I promise you I'll be fine."

Damn, seeing Cody stand up to her powerful grandfather, utterly calm, was a huge turn-on. Then again, the man just had to breathe to make her feel turned on and off-balance. She really had to have sex more often if this was the way she was going to react.

Callum and Cody stared each other down while Tinsley held her breath. Her grandfather was the first to cave. "Two months and it had better be a brilliant plan, Gallant," Callum muttered.

Cody one, Callum, zero, Tinsley thought. Cody and Callum shook hands and Callum moved toward the door. He yanked it open before turning back to look at them. He shook his head and winced. "This is either going to be a stroke of genius or you two will kill each other."

He wasn't wrong.

Four

On leaving the conference room, Cody told Tinsley that he'd see her in her office in fifteen minutes, that he had a couple of calls to make before he could give her his full attention.

He didn't bother asking whether she could meet with him, whether her schedule was flexible enough to accommodate him. No, he'd just assumed...

Irritating man.

Tinsley dropped into her chair behind her desk and pulled her oversize notepad toward her, flipping past the pages filled with colorful notations, reminders and shopping and to-do lists. Her notebook was part diary, part journal, and without it, she would be lost. Opening a blank page, she did what she always did when she was feeling overwhelmed and out of sorts: she made a list. But instead of making a list of everything she needed to do to give Callum a decent proposal, she found herself writing a list of why she shouldn't sleep with Cody again.

She didn't get further than "we don't like each other" and "we are now working together" when her computer beeped, the tone signaling an incoming personal message. She turned her attention to her screen and saw that the message was from JT. Tinsley frowned, wondering why her ex was contacting her. They hadn't spoken for almost as long as the divorce had been final…

Curious, her heart beating a little fast, she opened up the email and when she saw his first sentence— "Dear friends and family"—she knew she was part of a group message. She looked at the message recipients and saw that her parents, Kinga and Cody would also receive this missive. JT wasn't one for sending newsletters, so what prompted this?

One way to find out was to read on…

Hey everyone, just a quick note to tell you that Heather is pregnant. She's twenty weeks along and we're expecting a boy. We are ecstatic and can't wait to meet our little man.

Tinsley blinked, read the message again and shook her head. What the hell was he talking about? She read the message yet again. Right, it definitely said they were having a baby, but that made no sense to her. JT didn't want kids; he never had. Whenever she'd brought up the subject, he'd told her that he wasn't ready, that he didn't think he'd ever be ready. Kids weren't part of his plan...

They'd very much been a part of hers. She'd craved a child and, to be honest, she still did. She'd begged JT to give her a baby, for them to start their family but he'd continuously refused. Unusually, he couldn't be budged on the topic and he promised her that he'd never change his mind.

But he had. With someone else.

Tinsley wrapped her arms around her stomach and rocked in her chair, the news punching her over and over again. JT was going to be a dad, but she wasn't going to be a mom.

It was fundamentally wrong...

Tinsley stood up and walked over to her window, placing her hands on the glass and resting her forehead against the cold pane. She felt hot and cold, angry and soul-deep sad. JT and Heather were living her life, the picture-perfect life she'd planned. It wasn't fair...

She wasn't supposed to be alone, divorced, childless. According to her timeline, they should've had a house in the country by now and she'd be pregnant with child number two, possibly even child number three.

Tinsley heard the rap on her closed door, heard it open and, without looking up, lifted her finger telling whoever wanted a piece of her to wait. Before she faced anyone, she needed to get her raging emotions—fury and jealousy—under control.

Don't let them see you sweat...

She refused to let anyone see that she was upset, to see even a hint of tears. Whirling around and keeping her head down, she grabbed her phone and pretended to make a call, knowing she needed time to calm down, to get her emotions under control.

Masculine fingers removed her phone from her fingers and Tinsley reluctantly lifted her eyes, up and up some more, to look into Cody's harsh expression. Emotion, deep and sad, flashed in his eyes. "Ah, I take it you got the broadcast?"

She didn't need him to explain. "You got it too? You didn't know?" Tinsley demanded, resting her flat palms on the desk.

"JT and I don't talk anymore," Cody said. "That email came as much as a surprise to me as it did to you. I thought that, like me, JT never wanted kids."

Tinsley lifted her head to frown at him. "Why don't you want kids? How can you not want kids?"

His eyebrows rose at her demand and he shrugged. "My dad was a useless father, as was my grandfather. And, remember, I did raise JT from the time he was eight. I was a surrogate father far too early."

True. JT and Cody's dad had been so inactive in their lives that Tinsley could barely remember the man. He didn't attend any of JT's graduations, nor did he grace their wedding with his presence. He was more their bank manager than their father.

Cody gestured to her laptop screen and they both looked at the picture of Heather that JT had annoyingly included. Heather wore a tiny bikini and proudly showed off her baby bump, grinning into the camera. Tinsley narrowed her eyes before standing up and crossing her hands across her chest. She lifted her chin and her eyes slammed into Cody's.

"I want a baby," she abruptly stated.

Shock flashed across his face. "Uh… I'm not sure what I'm supposed to say to that."

Tinsley knew that her next words would be irrational but she could no more stop them than she could the sun rising in the east. "JT wouldn't give me a child—he refused to. He's now having a baby with someone else and *I want my own*."

"What?"

"I want my own child," Tinsley repeated. "Maybe I should get myself artificially inseminated using donor sperm."

Color leached from Cody's face. "What? You can't make decisions like that just because my idiot brother is expecting a child!"

"I wanted a child long before he did, since when we were first married. He refused to give me one!" Tinsley shouted. Why was she so quick to lose control of her words and emotions around Cody when keeping control was her thing? It was like she morphed into someone completely different around him…

Or someone more like herself. Tinsley pushed that thought away. "So, is this some weird competition between you and Heather?" Cody demanded.

Of course she wasn't competing…or maybe she was, just a little. She'd planned on having a little boy with JT's blond hair and sparkling green eyes. Or a little girl with her blue eyes and JT's nose. Tinsley cocked her head to the side, thinking that the brothers didn't look that different, except that Cody had darker hair and was bigger and taller. JT was smarter but Cody wasn't an academic slouch. Their DNA was pretty close…

Maybe she could still have a small piece of that original plan. Knowing that she was way off base, and possibly losing her damn mind, Tinsley allowed the words to come.

"Sleep with me again—give me a child."

Cody looked at her like she'd grown three heads and a tail. "No," Cody stated, taking two steps back.

She wasn't about to back down now. "Whether I get sperm from you or a donor, what's the difference? I'm not asking for anything but your DNA. That's *it.* I wouldn't expect you to be part of the kid's life, to pay for anything. This will be as anonymous as you want it to be."

He dragged his hand through his hair, his expression grim. "Tinsley, this is madness. The only reason you're suggesting this is that you're upset that JT and

Heather are having a baby, the baby you planned to have with him."

"He didn't want a child with me!" Tinsley shouted, mortified to feel tears on her cheeks. "He didn't want me!"

He moved fast and before she could react, his arms were around her and she was snuggled against his chest, her tears creating mascara streaks on his sweater. She put her fist to her mouth, and bit her knuckles, hoping to push her sobs away but they kept rising until they escaped.

She cried. For the first time ever, someone other than Kinga was witness to her distress and pain. And she didn't like it, not one bit.

She didn't like feeling this exposed, this vulnerable. Weak. Exposing her pressure points gave others the chance to hurt her. Tinsley was pretty sure she'd done enough hurting…

But JT's news stung. She felt like she'd never be whole again.

"My brother doesn't think," Cody murmured in her ear, his big hands drawing circles over her back. "He's got a massive brain but doesn't have the common sense God gave a gnat. He's not worth your tears."

"Oh, I know that! I'm not crying about him as much as about the life I lost, the one I planned. We were supposed to have a perfect life."

"There's no such thing, Tinsley!" Cody put his thumb under her chin and lifted her face so she had to look at him. "I understand this news rocked you, but you're upset and not thinking straight."

Truer words had never been spoken.

"And let me make this very clear, you are never getting my sperm."

She sniffed and wrinkled her nose. "If you change your mind, I'll take them. I'd much rather have your DNA than a random stranger's."

Cody's lips lifted a fraction. "Good to know but… *no*. You're not getting my boys, Tinsley. Not today, not ever."

"Damn," Tinsley muttered, dropping her head to rest her temple against his chest. She was so comfortable in his arms. She shouldn't be, but she was.

"Though I wouldn't be averse to sleeping with you again," Cody said from somewhere above her head.

Tinsley tensed and, leaving her hands on his chest, put a foot of space between them. She frowned, confused. "What?"

"You heard me," Cody told her, his thumb swiping away a tear on her left cheekbone. "I'd very much like to sleep with you again."

Tinsley felt her head spinning. This was all a bit much to take in. Her ex was having a baby, she'd asked his brother for his sperm, she'd cried and now Cody was hitting on her?

What. The. Hell?

"But…you are sleeping with Norah," Tinsley said, hoping to sound matter-of-fact. Since she sounded a little squeaky, she figured she'd overshot.

"I had a fling with Norah a few months ago and we made plans to meet up the night after you and I…" Cody hesitated. "I canceled our plans."

"Why?" Tinsley demanded.

"I didn't want her. I wanted you. I still do." Cody brushed her mouth with his and Tinsley found herself sinking into him, her arms going around his waist. He felt so solid, like a giant redwood that would never shift, no matter how strong the wind or the rain. He made her feel sexy, lovely and, best of all, alive.

Made her feel safe, secure, protected.

But she was making rainbows from rope again, confusing attraction with comfort or, even worse, she was looking for a distraction. She'd told herself that sleeping with Cody was a one-night deal.

She wasn't a have-some-fun-and-walk-away type of girl. Under her calm surface, she was too intense, too emotional. There were enough things in her life she wanted but couldn't have—a husband, a happy marriage, a baby or three—and she did not need to add Cody to that big, messy pile.

But it was hard to step back, nearly impossible to move out of the security of his big arms. It was so nice to feel protected. With JT, she was always the strong one, the one he leaned on, not the other way around.

But she needed to compose herself, to pull herself together. JT was having a kid. She had the right to feel regret, but she couldn't wallow in it. Using the heels of her hands, Tinsley rubbed her eyes, hoping she wasn't spreading her mascara everywhere, and pulled up a smile.

"I never have meltdowns and I'm sorry you had to witness me losing it."

Cody lifted his hands. "I think that was a very normal reaction to hearing unexpected news," he said.

She shrugged, embarrassed. "I reacted like that because she's getting to have what I wanted, the one thing I still want." She nodded decisively. "At some point, I'm going to have a baby. Hopefully sooner rather than later."

She placed her hands on her stomach and pulled in a deep breath. "Can you give me ten minutes to wash my face? And then I think we should get to work. We've got a lot to do."

"Are you sure you're okay?" Cody asked her, sliding his hands into the pockets of his pants, "Maybe you should take the rest of the day off and we can come back to Ryder International business tomorrow?"

He'd never suggest that if she were a man. No, he'd expect his male colleague to dust off his emotions and carry on. And because Tinsley couldn't, *wouldn't*, give herself any slack, that was exactly what she did.

But only after she spent the next ten minutes repairing her makeup in her private bathroom.

Cody paced the long, thin balcony dotted with chairs and tables outside the Ryder International break room and told himself to control his temper.

He reminded himself, for the tenth time, that tossing his phone from seventeen floors was not an option.

He was relatively easygoing, but his younger brother had the knack of cranking the heat under his temper. While waiting for Tinsley to compose herself earlier, he'd video-called JT in Hong Kong.

JT answered on the first ring. "I thought my news would warrant a call from you," he said, smirking.

They hadn't exchanged more than brief Christmas and birthday phone calls for more than two years. On hearing that JT abandoned Tinsley, Cody had flown to Hong Kong to have it out with his brother, who didn't seem to care that he'd left a heartbroken wife behind. He had a new life; the old one was behind him. Then, like today, it was all about JT and how he felt.

"You didn't think that maybe you should've called Tinsley and told her privately before you told everyone else that you're having a baby?" Cody asked him, trying to keep a lid on his temper.

"Why?" JT asked, sounding genuinely confused.

"It's a respect thing, JT," Cody replied, gripping the bridge of his nose. "I gather that she desperately wanted a child, but you refused."

"I didn't want a baby with her, but I do want one with Heather," JT replied. When Cody just stared at him, he shrugged. "This isn't rocket science, Cody. Tinsley is my past. Heather is my future. She's my everything."

"You cheated on Tinsley, abandoned her, destroyed

her dreams of having a family and then you drop the news that you are having a kid in a generic email. She deserves more than that, JT!"

"We're divorced, it's over and I don't care how she feels. I have a new life. Why can't you understand that?" JT demanded.

JT was more like their father than Cody had imagined. As long as he was happy, as long as he was doing what he wanted to do, life was fine. Taking responsibility and considering feelings other than his own were not traits he possessed.

It was all about him, all the time.

Arguing with JT was a waste of time. His brother was a selfish prick and probably always would be. He'd caused Tinsley a lot of pain and maybe if he had expressed some contrition, Cody might have been able to forgive him. But he hadn't and Cody was over making excuses for him.

"Aren't you going to congratulate me, big brother?"

"Yeah, congrats," Cody replied, keeping his voice flat and uninterested.

JT was so wrapped up in himself he didn't hear Cody's lack of enthusiasm. When JT started to talk about birth plans—they were thinking about flying in a famous doula from Greece for her to assist Heather because she was determined to have a home birth—Cody decided he'd heard enough. He ended the call.

He heard footsteps behind him and turned to see Kinga approaching him. Tinsley's older sister looked a little frazzled and he presumed she'd also heard the news.

"What's a doula?" he demanded.

Kinga wrinkled her nose. "A doula is a midwife." She rested her arms on the balcony railing and shivered as a cold wind blew across the harbor and up the side of the building. "I was on my way to Tinsley, but saw you standing out here. Is she okay?"

Cody rocked his right hand from side to side. "She's mad, hurt, upset. She keeps saying she wants a baby."

Kinga didn't look surprised. "She's always wanted kids, from the time she was little. She pretended all her dolls were babies. She wanted to go off the pill when she left high school but promised JT she'd wait until they graduated college. When she raised the subject again, he told her he didn't want kids, and, not trusting her to take care of contraception, started using condoms when they made love."

Cody winced at Kinga's words. "My brother is a douche."

"Yep, he is. I think Tins wanted a baby more than she wanted a husband, so this news will hit her hard."

"She cried a little," Cody admitted.

"Tinsley cried?" Kinga grabbed his arm and dug her nails into the fabric above his skin. "She never cries! In fact, I'm surprised she even let on she was upset. Tinsley keeps her emotions hidden."

Yeah, he knew that and he hated it. "She was pretty upset."

So upset that she'd asked him for his sperm. The thought made him feel squirrelly and weird, jumpy.

"I'll go and talk to her," Kinga said, her eyes worried.

Cody shook his head. "She's calm now and she's expecting me any minute. Leave her and let her get back to work."

Kinga didn't look convinced. "I think she needs me, Cody."

The sisters had a rock-steady bond. "She always needs you, Kinga, but maybe you can chat with her later? She wants to work now, and God knows, we have a lot of it to do."

Kinga eventually nodded. "That's not a lie. What the hell was Callum thinking demanding a proposal in such little time? I swear, that old man…" she muttered.

Cody placed his hand on Kinga's back and ushered her to the door. They stepped into warmth and Cody headed for the state-of-the-art coffee machine, asking Kinga if she wanted some. She said yes and told Cody Tinsley would prefer a hot chocolate and how to make it for her.

"Is Callum okay?" Cody asked, remembering Callum's pale face and earlier ornery attitude. "He was pretty abrupt earlier."

"Have you met my grandfather?" Kinga demanded, placing her elbows on a high table next to the coffee station. "He's always abrupt, some would say blatantly rude."

That was true. "He just seemed worse than usual, and he doesn't look that well," Cody commented. "His hand was shaking."

"I didn't notice," Kinga admitted. "I know he's mad because there's been some sort of delay on the DNA tests he requested at Christmas."

Kinga went on to explain how their DNA would be entered into a genealogy website, that the family could find out where they came from originally and whether they had any distant relatives scattered throughout the world.

"He's obsessed with his bloodline and wants the results. But DNA testing has become quite popular, the lab is backed up and Callum doesn't like waiting." Kinga took the coffee he held out and blew across the liquid before taking a sip. "My parents are also acting weird, by the way."

Callum fixed Tinsley's hot chocolate. "How?"

"They're both grumpy, both snappy, both tense. Tins and I are presently avoiding them as much as possible."

"Your dad was his normal charming self this morning," Cody commented.

"Where do you think Tins inherited her acting ability from, Cody? She and Dad can both be dying inside but nobody would suspect it." She frowned. "That's why I'm so very surprised she cried in front of you. You're not one of her favorite people."

Her words punched him in the gut. "I know. But I'm hoping that will change…" He saw the speculation on Kinga's face and thought he'd better nip any ideas jumping into her head. "We need to work together, Kinga, and it would be easier if we managed to be friends."

Kinga narrowed her eyes at him. "Are you sure that's it?"

Cody picked up his and Tinsley's mugs and sent her a bland smile. "What else could it be, Kinga?"

Before she could answer, he strode away and headed back toward Tinsley's office, thinking that he never experienced this much drama at his place. Life around the Ryder-Whites was never boring.

Five

Five weeks later, in the bathroom of her hotel room in Manhattan, Tinsley stared at the pregnancy test lying facedown on the vanity, her heart beating as fast as a hummingbird's wings.

The words *be careful what you wish for* flashed across her brain and she thought she heard a witch's cackle coming from a long distance away. Her period was three weeks late and, since she was ridiculously regular, the most obvious conclusion was that she was pregnant. Courtesy of her ex-husband's brother.

Dear Lord.

The test, two pink lines, would confirm her suspicions but she couldn't bring herself to flip it over. She'd given the idea of being a single mom some thought since receiving JT's blasé email, but she never once thought she might be pregnant herself.

Cody used condoms and condoms were ninety-nine percent effective, weren't they? She couldn't be pregnant; there was no way. She was just late because she'd been working so hard and was so stressed. Tinsley placed a hand on her stomach, pushed the tips of her fingers into her skin and shook her head. No, her carrying a child didn't make sense, didn't feel right.

Her being pregnant didn't resonate.

She glanced at the test again and shook her head. She'd just ignore the test for now, Tinsley decided, looking at her reflection in the mirror above the vanity. If she flipped it over and saw only one stripe, she'd be disappointed. If she saw two, she'd be terrified, and she didn't think she could hide either emotion. She didn't want to attend the Ryder International Valentine's Ball looking shell-shocked.

Tinsley turned and looked at herself in the long, vertical mirror behind the door. She wore a white sheath, designed by Prada. The entire outfit, and her decency, depended on a thin cord running from her right shoulder down her back to her left hip, leaving most of her back bare. A high slit left her left thigh exposed and showed off her sparkly Jimmy Choos. The dress was stark and sleek and her stylist recommended a halo braid and low bun, long curtain bangs framing her face and soft, natural makeup to contrast the severity of the dress. It worked, Tinsley decided; she looked…reasonable.

While she couldn't do anything about the worry in her eyes, at least her expertly applied makeup gave her some color. She placed her hands over her flat stomach and closed her eyes, feeling overwhelmed. How was she supposed to go to a ball, smile and flirt and laugh, while she still didn't know what was on that stick?

Maybe she should just check it…

If it says yes, you'll be thrown into a tailspin. If it says no, you'll be gutted. No, it was better to stay in limbo until the ball was over. She could cry, scream or panic after the ball when she was alone.

Her phone beeped with a message and Tinsley picked it up. It was Kinga, telling her that her family was waiting outside the Forrester-Grantham Ballroom and their guests were arriving. Where the hell was she?

Wincing, Tinsley picked up the pregnancy test and shoved it into her small clutch bag, forcing it in so that it lay from corner to corner. Lipstick went down one side, and her hotel key card on the other side. She didn't have room for her phone, but that didn't matter, since she would be with her family tonight. Not bothering to check her reflection again, she left the room and hurried down the hallway to the bank of elevators.

She just had to get through the evening, and she could fall apart later. She breathed deeply as the elevator descended and opened onto the floor housing the ornate ballroom. She pulled a practiced smile onto her face and walked toward her family, holding her dress so the hem didn't catch on her spiky heels or skim the floor.

Her eyes went to her sister, who looked stunning in a deep red ball gown, her smile as bright as the diamond glittering on the ring finger of her left hand. Kinga had spent a lot of time with Griff O'Hare over the past six weeks and had fallen in love with the reformed bad boy of rock and roll, who was also the ball's headline act. Tinsley kissed her parents and greeted Callum before placing her cheek against Kinga's and inhaling her sister's gorgeous scent.

"You look great, King," Tinsley told her, her lips close to Kinga's ear. "You're glowing."

Kinga squeezed her hands and Tinsley stepped back. "*You* look amazing, Tins. I love your dress," Kinga told her, placing her arm in hers and leading her away from the family, who'd turned to greet a Bahraini princess. "Callum and the parents can hold down the fort and greet the guests. We are going to take a minute for ourselves."

They approached a waiter holding a tray of champagne and Kinga picked up two glasses and handed one to Tinsley. They clinked, Tinsley took a small sip—surely a half glass wouldn't hurt her baby, if there even *was* a baby—and wrinkled her nose.

"What's wrong?" Kinga asked her, her eyes narrowing.

"Nothing, the champagne just tastes a little weird." It shouldn't; it was Krug Clos du Mesnil

Blanc de Blancs, the '95 vintage, and it cost over a grand a bottle.

"No, it doesn't," Kinga replied, taking another sip. "It's utterly delicious."

Tinsley shrugged. "I've just brushed my teeth, so that's probably why. Where's Griff?"

Kinga's eyes softened. "With his band doing bandy things. I watched his dress rehearsal today and he's going to be brilliant."

"Of course he is," Tinsley told her, smiling. She liked Kinga's man partly because he was a nice guy, but mostly because he made her sister so damn happy.

Kinga nudged her and fanned her face. "Wow. If I was single…"

Tinsley turned to look at the trio of men stepping out of the elevator. She couldn't help her little sigh. Garrett Kaye—über-wealthy venture capitalist and the son of Callum's assistant, Emma—was the tallest of the three, topping out at six-five. He wore his light brown hair short and his beard was new and tinged with red. She recognized Sutton Marchant, previously an international stockbroker, now an author. He and Garrett seemed to be on friendly terms, Tinsley presumed they knew each other from the world of finance. Sutton shared the same coloring as Tinsley, dark hair and blue eyes, except that Sutton's eyes were a lot lighter and more arresting.

Tinsley looked at Cody, her lungs immediately forgetting how to suck air. As she could now attest,

Cody Gallant looked his best wearing only his birthday suit, but he also, damn him, rocked a tuxedo. She
took in the details. His suit was designer with narrow, grosgrain notch lapels matching his flat-front
pants and his vest. His shirt was a crisp and classic
white, with a plain front style and a perfectly knot-
ted bow tie.

He looked fantastic.

Cody noticed her, lifted a hand in acknowledg-
ment, turning his head to look past Garrett's shoulder. His sexy face broke out into a grin. Tinsley
looked to see who'd grabbed his attention and sighed.
She couldn't blame Cody; she always smiled whenever she saw her best friend too. Not only was Jules
beautiful—her looks courtesy of her Swedish and
Mauritian ancestry—she was also funny, supersmart
and outgoing. And, as one of the world's best mixologists, she would be one of the main judges for their
cocktail competition.

Tinsley watched as Cody enveloped her gorgeous
friend in a huge hug and then introduced her to Garrett and Sutton. Cody kept a loose arm around Jules,
and Tinsley felt a burning sensation in her stomach
move up to her chest.

Kinga jammed her elbow into Tinsley's side. "Did
you just growl?" she demanded.

She had, but there was no way on earth she'd
admit that. Or that she was jealous of the attention
Jules was receiving from Cody. Jules was her best
friend, *dammit*, and as far as she knew, there was

nothing but friendship between her and Cody. And even if there was, it shouldn't be a problem.

Unless she was pregnant… Then things might become complicated.

You are such a liar, Tinsley Tamlyn Ryder-White. You'd hate it if he and Jules hooked up.

God. Her grip tightened on her glass and she was sure enamel was flying off her teeth from grinding them together so hard. This evening was going to last six hundred hours, and she wasn't even twenty minutes in.

She wanted to go upstairs, climb under the covers and hide out for a while. From Cody, from life and most definitely from reality.

And from that damn test.

Standing at the bar, watching Garrett Kaye arguing with Jules Carlson, James noticed Garrett's eyes were so like Callum's—a deep, dark blue—and they flashed with irritation. But under the annoyance was a healthy dose of amusement and enjoyment.

Like Callum, Garrett wasn't used to people arguing with him. James thought that having a spirited discussion with a fiery woman would do Garrett some good. He needed a challenge and Jules was just the person to give him a run for his money.

James's son—unacknowledged but still his—was ruthless and arrogant and needed to be brought down a peg or two. Few people, so he'd heard, were allowed inside Garrett's inner world. Even Emma, his mom, was encouraged to keep her emotional distance.

James sighed. If anyone, particularly Callum, found out Garrett was his son and Callum's grandson, everything that was to come to James—stocks, shares, art, cash and properties—would go to Garrett. James didn't want that to happen. He'd done what he could for Garrett, he'd anonymously bequeathed him a trust fund when he turned twenty-one, but Tinsley and Kinga were his legitimate children. They carried the Ryder-White name and had put up with Callum all their lives.

Besides, Garrett was as wealthy as Callum and Callum's inheritance would be an excess of riches.

Garrett's head whipped up and their eyes connected. He lifted a sardonic eyebrow, said something to Jules, hopefully excusing himself, and turned to walk in James's direction, his expression mocking. He slid into the empty spot next to James, rested his elbows on the bar and ordered a fifteen-year-old whiskey.

"Care to tell me why you're watching me?" Garrett demanded.

Straight to the point, James thought. He scrambled for an answer. "I've known Jules for a long time, she's Tinsley's best friend and I'm protective of her."

"And you think she needs protection from me?"

James nodded. "Something like that."

"Bullshit," Garrett retorted. "Firstly, Jules needs no help. Her tongue is more effective than industrial-strength paint stripper. And you weren't looking at her—you were looking at me."

It took all of James's willpower to keep his expression impassive. "If you say so," he said, allowing a trace of derision to touch his voice. It was a trick he'd learned from Callum and one that was normally effective.

Garrett wasn't even a little chastised. He simply sipped his whiskey and looked over his glass at James. "Why have I caught your attention, James? Why am I in your crosshairs?"

James swallowed. It wasn't easy to see your son look at you with such a derisive expression.

"Whenever I'm around you, I get the feeling that you can affect me, or my life, in some way," Garrett continued.

James fought to keep his face impassive, unable to speak past the lump in his throat. Then Garrett's voice dropped again and turned menacing. "Why do I sense that you, the son of my mother's boss, has the ability to upend my life?"

"Maybe your Spidey sense is wrong," James suggested, his words weak.

"It's never wrong," Garrett retorted, banging his glass on the bar. He looked down at James, his eyes dark and dangerous. "What's going on, James? What are you thinking, planning? Want to save me the hassle and tell me now?"

James kept his tongue behind his teeth as sweat ran down his back. His son, this man, was tough and took no prisoners. He doubted that he would welcome being told of his parentage during one of the world's most exclusive balls.

And James had promised Emma he'd never reveal his true identity. And he knew that if he did, he and his legitimate family would lose everything. "I think you've either had too much to drink or have an overactive imagination, Garrett."

Garrett shook his head. "Nah, that's not it." Garrett clamped his hand around James's shoulder and squeezed. "You don't have to tell me. I'm good at ferreting out secrets and I'll discover yours."

That's what I'm afraid of, James thought as Garrett strode away.

Griff O'Hare was three songs in and Tinsley, sitting across the overly decorated table from Cody, looked as green as the pistachio ice cream on her plate. Not that she'd eaten any. Neither had she taken one bite from the previous five courses; she'd simply pushed her food around.

If he ignored the pallor in her cheeks, she looked sensational. And her dress, held up by nothing more than a thin cord, was the sexiest in the room. She looked, with her messy up-do and smoky eyes, fantastic but he could see beyond the styling to know that something was wrong with his once off lover and current colleague.

She looked like the weight of the world was sitting on her shoulders. And the fact that he didn't know who or what was causing her such distress pissed him off. He'd known her since she was a kid and he could read her better than he could read most. Something was eating her from the inside out and he wanted to know what it was so he could fix it for her.

She's not yours to fix, Gallant, and you don't do that shit anymore, remember?

Cody sighed and tapped his finger against the crystal tumbler holding his shot of excellent whiskey. Griff was singing an old, popular standard and all eyes, including Tinsley's, were on the superstar. Except for Cody's. He couldn't pull his eyes off Tinsley.

What was wrong with her?

She'd been tired lately, but that wasn't unexpected. They'd both been working crazy long days trying to keep up with their current work schedules while also compiling the proposal for the cocktail competition.

If Callum approved their project, plans and budget—and his fee—he and Tinsley would spend the next few months putting their plans into action before she handed over the nitty-gritty day-to-day operation to the team he'd yet to select.

But until then, their workdays would become longer. If Tinsley wasn't coping now, she wouldn't cope in a couple of weeks.

It didn't help that she was so into control and couldn't ask for help. She made life ten times harder for herself than it needed to be. But she never complained, was ludicrously efficient and he never saw her lose her cool. He wished she would. Seeing the very uptight Tinsley Ryder-White losing it would be quite fun.

Since her mini-meltdown in her office after hearing JT's baby news, tonight was the first time he'd seen her looking less than picture-perfect. Was she sick? Stressed? Feeling overwhelmed?

But, because she was as even-keeled as ever, how the hell would he ever know?

Judging by the professional way Tinsley treated him, nobody would suspect that they'd had intense, amazing, jaw-dropping sex six weeks ago. She was polite, direct and completely focused on the task at hand. When he'd tried to talk about anything other than work, whether it was politics or the ball or her family, she always cut him off and turned the subject back to business.

Tinsley was determined to pretend they hadn't spent the first hours of the New Year naked and yet he couldn't forget it. The entire night had been burned on his memory and he hadn't been able to accept any invitations for bed-based fun from Norah or anyone else.

One night with his ex-sister-in-law had totally screwed up his sex life. And, strangely, he was okay with that. He didn't want a relationship but casual sex had lost its appeal. Which left him dating himself...

But if Tinsley crooked her little finger, he'd be out of this chair so damn fast...

Cody picked up his glass and tossed his whiskey back, enjoying the burn. He tuned back in to Sutton and Garrett's conversation. They were talking about a new cryptocurrency taking the world by storm. Cody remembered that Sutton had been an investment banker before he'd hit the nonfiction bestseller list with an easy-to-digest guide to stocks and shares. He'd then switched to writing fiction and his blood-soaked books regularly hit the bestseller lists.

During a lull in the conversation, Jules, who was sitting between him and Garrett, looked across to Tinsley. "I'm looking forward to being involved in the cocktail competition as a judge, Tins. It's such a great idea."

"It was my dad's idea," Tinsley told her, pushing away her untouched dessert plate.

Jules took a sip of champagne, her eyebrows pulled into a thin line. "I saw that Crazy Kate's Gin is listed as one of the companies you're going to ask to sponsor the competition."

Tinsley nodded. "Yeah, they've been one of our most important suppliers for decades."

Jules winced. "I don't know if they're going to come on board, Tins. They're laying off their employees and scaling down their operations."

"What?" Tinsley demanded, shocked. "But why?"

Jules looked a little green. "So many factors, including the effect of the COVID pandemic."

Cody noticed that both Garrett and Sutton were tuned in to their conversation. "Crazy Kate's is the one based in North Carolina, right?" Cody asked, racking his brain.

"No, it's a Colorado company," Jules corrected him. "I feel sick about it. Crazy Kate's was the first company I did promotions for. Kate herself suggested that I do pop-up bars. She was instrumental in getting my business off the ground. Ryder's and Crazy Kate's did a joint promotion and that's how I met Tinsley and Kinga."

Garrett spoke, his deep voice cutting through the buzz of the room. "They recently upgraded their bottling plant, right? And built a brand-new distribution depot?"

Cody shook his head, astounded by Garrett's encyclopedic knowledge of the world of business. He was famous as being one of the country's best venture capitalists, investing in companies exhibiting high growth potential.

But nothing about Garrett was simple. The guy also ran a lucrative vulture capital fund, doing the exact opposite. If he saw the opportunity to buy a business debt from a bank or a lending institution, and sell that debt or take over company assets to repay that debt, he'd do that too. Garrett was a corporate shark.

Jules pointed her spoon in Garrett's direction. "Do not go anywhere near them, Kaye," she told him, her expression fierce. Right, so Jules also knew of Garrett's darker dealings. Nothing he did was illegal, Cody admitted, but some of his decisions were morally questionable.

Garrett lifted his hands in mock surrender. "What? I just asked an innocent question!"

Jules told him that even as a baby, he'd never been innocent and Cody leaned back in his seat, entertained by their argument. Jules wasn't a fool and she wasn't intimidated by the very powerful, very taciturn Garrett Kaye. Good for her.

Cody looked at Tinsley to see how she was reacting to the heated argument entertaining him and Sutton but she'd stood up, her face as pale as her white dress. Her eyes connected with his and she briefly shook her head. Within seconds she was flying across the ballroom... Hell, he didn't think a woman could walk so fast in high heels.

Something was wrong...

He looked at Jules but she was still arguing with Garrett and hadn't noticed Tinsley leaving. He looked around for Kinga but she was standing next to the stage. Griff was on his haunches with his hand cupping her face as he sang to her.

They were together? Okay, surprising but not important right now.

Tinsley's mom... Where was Penelope? Cody saw that Penelope and Callum were talking to the Senate majority leader, one of the most powerful people in Washington. They were out...

That left him. Brilliant.

Cody pushed his chair back, excused himself from the table—only Sutton acknowledged his leaving— and followed Tinsley's path. He left the busy ballroom, stepped into the lobby and looked around. She would've headed for the elevators or the ladies' room and, judging by her speed, he bet on the latter.

Sighing, Cody headed for the room, walked down the L-shaped hallway and stepped into a beautifully decorated room, complete with a two-seater sofa covered in pink-and-black stripes and gilded mirrors. He quickly noted that only one stall, the nearest one, was occupied. The door was half-open and through the opening, he saw a sliver of white silk.

And then he heard the sound of retching…

Shit! Thinking quickly, Cody closed the main door leading into the room and flipped the lock. Whoever needed to use the facilities could hold it or find another bathroom.

Returning to the stall, he gently pushed open the door to see Tinsley on her bare knees in front of the bowl, swaying as she tried to hold her hair back and keep her balance.

Unfazed, Cody gathered her hair in his big hand and dropped beside her, slinging his free arm behind her waist to keep her steady. "I've got you, babe."

Tinsley whipped her head around to scowl at him. "Do. Not. Call. Me. Babe. And go away," she told him before her body reacted with another spasm.

No chance in hell. Especially since she was leaning against him, relying on him to keep her upright. Under his hand, he felt the heat of her skin and the ripples of her still-contracting stomach.

He hoped she didn't have a stomach bug. He

wasn't worried about catching it himself—he had the constitution of an ox—but Tinsley was too thin already. She couldn't afford to lose any more weight. Tinsley rested her head against his shoulder and he placed his hand against her forehead. She was cool, thank God, she didn't seem to be running a fever.

"Better?" he asked, tucking a strand of sweet-smelling hair behind her ear.

Tinsley nodded.

"Then can I lift you off this disgusting floor?" To be fair, it was sparkling clean but she had to want to get up off her knees. Tinsley held onto him as he lifted her onto her feet, her dress falling to the floor. He held her hips, not prepared to let her go until he was very certain she was okay on those ice-pick heels.

Her balance steadied, but she still looked like death warmed up. Cody ushered her out of the stall and led her over to the striped couch. "Sit down and I'll go and find you a bottle of water so you can rinse out your mouth."

Tinsley sank to the couch and shook her head. "I didn't actually throw up. I just went through the motions."

"Okay. But sick or not, you still look like crap," Cody told her, pushing back his jacket to put his hands on his hips. "Did you eat something strange for lunch?"

"No, it's nothing I ate." Tinsley looked up at him, her blue eyes holding a hint of purple. In them, he saw a swirl of emotions, with fear and trepidation leading the charge.

"Then what the hell is wrong with you?"

"I think it's this." Tinsley opened her clutch bag and tugged out a plastic stick, which she handed to him. He flipped it over and saw two pink stripes in a tiny window. He was old enough to know what a pregnancy test looked like and what two stripes meant. "Shit! You're pregnant?"

Tinsley reached for the stick, took it and stared down at the lines. "Seems so."

"You didn't know?" Cody demanded, feeling like he'd stepped into a complicated film with dizzying plot changes.

"I took the test earlier, but I didn't look at it. I couldn't," she explained, pushing her fingers into her hair and dislodging more strands. "But throwing up was a big clue."

"How far along are you?" Cody demanded, his eyes going to her still-flat stomach.

"Six weeks or so," Tinsley replied. Her words were accompanied by her lifted eyebrows and a searching look and Cody frowned, thinking that there was a subtext here that he was missing.

"What?" he demanded. "Just...*what*?"

"Six weeks ago was New Year's Eve, Cody, and what were we doing that night?"

He didn't...what...huh?

Tinsley rolled her eyes, obviously exasperated by his lack of understanding. "Do you need me to draw you a picture, Gallant? You and I slept together, which means that you are my baby's daddy."

Cody placed a hand on his stomach, looked back toward the stall and thought there was a good chance his dinner might make a comeback too.

Six

After she dropped her bombshell, neither of them had any interest in returning to the ball. They headed to the elevator and Cody jabbed the button to take them up to his private suite, the one the hotel owners kept for visiting friends and family. Not only was he a college friend of Fox Forrester, heir to the Forrester-Grantham fortune and the group's current CEO, but he'd also staged some of the hotel's most exclusive events.

Cody was a fixture in this hotel and had permanent access to the suite. The elevator ride up was quick and silent and the hallway leading to his suite was empty, thank God. Cody punched in the code on the door and gestured for Tinsley to step inside.

A foot in and the motion sensor lights flickered on and bathed the hallway in soft, calming light.

Good, they needed calm. More than that, he needed a drink. A big one.

Cody walked into the exquisite penthouse, located on the east corner of the hotel. It had one of the best views in the city, with panoramic views of the Hudson River, the city and Central Park. The suite was over two floors, and the second floor sported two huge bedrooms with oversize windows, wonderful views of downtown Manhattan and en-suite bathrooms with Italian-marble surfaces, huge showers and large soaking tubs.

But as exquisitely decorated as the rooms were, with amazing artwork, handblown glass sculptures and designer furniture, Tinsley's words from earlier kept bouncing around his brain.

You are my baby's daddy...

Holy, holy hell. Cody ran his hands over his face and headed for the drinks trolley in the corner, automatically reaching for a crystal decanter. He sloshed some whiskey into a short tumbler and tossed it back, immediately refilling his glass and tossing back another shot.

It couldn't be possible. He didn't understand. This had to be a joke.

Holding onto the glass, he turned to see Tinsley standing in the middle of the lounge, still looking like a wraith in her white dress and tumbled-down hair. "For God's sake sit down before you fall down," he ordered.

He saw the flash of defiance in her eyes but then she sighed, sat down and pulled off her heels, curling her feet under her butt and leaning her head back. She'd just imparted rock-his-world news, but his fingers still ached with the need to touch. He desperately wanted his mouth on hers, to be skin on skin, heart to heart.

God, maybe there was something wrong with him.

"Can I get you something to drink?" he asked. "Whiskey? Wine? A liqueur?"

Tinsley wrinkled her nose. "Since I'm officially with child, I shouldn't drink."

Right. Hell.

"A lemonade would be great," Tinsley replied, her eyes drifting closed. She inched down and turned on her side and Cody suspected she was a couple of deep breaths away from falling asleep.

"Don't go to sleep," he told her. "We have to talk."

"I'm still going to be pregnant in the morning," Tinsley protested. "I'm exhausted, Cody, let me sleep. Just for fifteen minutes and then you can wake me up."

"We're going to talk, *now*," Cody stated, his voice hard as stone. He walked over to the hidden fridge, opened it and pulled out a bottled lemonade. Grabbing a glass from the cupboard, he twisted off the cap, poured the liquid over some ice and walked back to her, pushing the glass into her hand. "Sit up and drink this. The sugar should pick you up."

Tinsley scowled at his bossy order. But she did sit up and take a few sips. Cody sat down on the coffee table in front of her, placed his arms on his knees and linked his hands together.

"Start from the beginning," he told her.

Tinsley sipped and shrugged. "There's not much to say. We slept together, one of your boys met one of my girls and here we are."

Cody pinched the bridge of this nose. "We used condoms, Tinsley. Every single time."

"And condoms are only ninety-eight percent effective," Tinsley snapped back. She banged her glass down on the table. Cody, feeling hot, shrugged out of his jacket. He ripped off his bow tie, undid the top buttons on his shirt and opened the buttons on his vest. He also picked up the remote for the air conditioner and dropped the temperature of the room.

He was in danger of overheating. Possibly exploding.

"The condom could've been damaged, had a microtear or you could've put it on wrong!" she added.

Cody glared at her. "I've been using condoms for a damn long time, Tinsley. I know how to put one on." His heart in his throat, he remembered their conversation about JT and his baby, just a week after they slept together. She told him she desperately wanted a baby, that she'd wanted one for a long, long time. She had asked him for his sperm. Maybe she'd set him up on New Year's Eve; maybe this had all been planned.

Or maybe, because she was pissed that Heather was having a kid and she wasn't, she'd hooked up with someone else without using protection, got lucky and decided to pin fatherhood on him.

"Is there a possibility that I'm not the father, Tinsley?" he asked, his voice freezer cold.

Tinsley took a moment to make sense of his question and Cody watched, fascinated as fire flared in her eyes. "What?"

"I know how much you want a baby, so I'm not taking this at face value." He looked down at the test. "These things are pretty sensitive these days. You could've hooked up with someone else and be two weeks pregnant for all I know."

God, that sounded so harsh, but he was looking for an escape hatch.

Tinsley lifted her finger, opened her mouth and closed it again. Then she jabbed a long nail into his thigh. "Are you accusing me of lying, of trying to pin this on you, Gallant?"

He didn't answer her, but neither did he look away.

"I don't need to lie! I am financially independent and completely able to raise a child on my own. I don't need you and I would *never* say you were the father if you weren't! How dare you suggest such a thing?"

Oh, he dared. "So, you're telling me that I'm the only one you've been with in the last couple of months?"

Tinsley tossed her hands up in the air. "You're the only person I've been with since JT!"

Oh…but…wow. Until he came along, this vibrant, passionate, sensual woman hadn't had sex for nearly three years? Possibly longer than that? Holy crap.

Cody rubbed his hands over his face, trying to scrub away his confusion. She was gorgeous and sexy and she had to have had offers. He told her as much.

"Offers I refused," Tinsley retorted. "Why are we discussing my sex life when we should be talking about that?"

He followed her gaze to the pregnancy test he still held in his hand. He swallowed, mentally hearing the jail doors clanging closed. He was trapped, and panic started to build in his throat. "I can't be the father, Tinsley. There's no way. I'm sorry, but you have to be wrong."

After raising JT, Cody had designed his life to avoid being personally responsible for anyone other than himself. Now she was telling him he had a baby on the way, a helpless infant for whom he'd be responsible for…the rest of his life? Tinsley swung her feet off the couch and reached for her shoes, sliding one, then the other onto her elegant feet.

"I didn't think anything could top you telling me not to marry JT on the night before our wedding, Cody, but your asinine reaction has just proved me wrong." She pulled the pregnancy wand from his closed fist and lifted her nose, eyeing him as she would gum stuck to her shoe.

"I am going to speak in short sentences and use small words so that this penetrates…

"I am six weeks pregnant, and this baby was conceived the night we slept together." She stood up and bent down to pick up her clutch bag. When she straightened, her cheeks were red with temper. "Forget this night, forget this conversation, forget that your sperm met my egg. As far as I'm concerned, you're a sperm donor and I want nothing more to do with you."

"We're going to be working together for the next few months, at least," Cody told her, knowing that was an indisputable fact.

"I would rather resign than work with you, Gallant. Stay away from me. Far, far away."

Cody watched as she stormed out of the lounge, into the hallway and out the door. He heard the door slam behind her and winced.

That didn't go well.

And that was the understatement of the year.

Heads up, Cody Gallant is on his way to see you.

Tinsley was working from home today. In her sitting room on Congress Street, she scowled at the message from her assistant before dropping the phone onto her coffee table. Moose, her massive Maine coon cat, lay over her feet and she'd lost feeling in her right foot ten minutes ago. But Moose tended to nip when disturbed so she'd left him alone.

Steeling herself, she whipped her legs out from under his solid body and narrowly missed having teeth marks on her toe.

"You're a fiend," Tinsley muttered, standing up. Her foot buckled and she yelped as tingles shot through her appendage and she spent the next minute dancing around, waiting for blood to return to her foot.

It gave her something else to think about other than Cody Gallant, who would, any minute, arrive at her doorstep. Nearly a week had passed since she'd dropped her life-changing news on the guy, and she'd been ducking his calls ever since.

On Monday, she went to London to talk to a British ad agency about a new TV advertisement and stayed a couple days longer than necessary. She could've held the meeting over Skype but since she was trying to avoid Cody, getting out of the country seemed a reasonable, albeit expensive, option.

She'd returned yesterday to another barrage of emails and a dozen missed calls from him. Cody was running out of patience, and Tinsley realized that she couldn't avoid him forever. At some point, they'd have to discuss her pregnancy and what she expected from him—nothing—and how involved he intended to be in her, and her child's life—not at all.

Her child's life...

Why didn't that phrase make her want to dance on the spot, bubble with anticipation? She'd always wanted to be a mother and couldn't wait to be pregnant, to meet and raise her child. She'd spent many hours dreaming about being pregnant, growing bigger, giving life but instead of feeling excited, all she felt was...blah. Even indifferent.

What was wrong with her?

Sure, she was upset about Cody's reaction, but she should still be thrilled to be pregnant. But she wasn't.

And she didn't know why not.

She was equally unexcited about seeing Cody but reluctantly admitted that they needed to have a, hopefully, rational conversation to figure out a way to work together going forward. Because that was today's other big news: yesterday Callum approved their plans for the cocktail competition and had given them the final budget, more generous than she'd expected. Now they had to work together to take it from paper to reality.

Tinsley glanced down at her clothes and winced. She was dressed in yoga pants and a slouchy moss green sweater. Her hair was piled up on her head and anchored by a big crocodile clip. After conversing with the porcelain god in her bathroom earlier, she'd showered, brushed her teeth and slapped some moisturizer on her face. Then she'd gone back to bed and slept for an hour.

Surely being this tired and this sick—she had morning sickness all day and all night—wasn't normal. But all the literature she'd read assured her that some women had awful first trimesters. Maybe she was feeling so disconnected from her pregnancy because her body was being utterly uncooperative. Her insane work schedule and her inconvenient, can't-stop-thinking-about-him attraction to the baby's father added to her stress and didn't they say that the body was a reflection of the mind?

And, let's be honest, her mind was a mess.

Walking over to her window, she looked out on

the snow-dusted lawn and saw Cody's luxury Mercedes SUV swing into her driveway. She'd hoped
to have time to change into something a little more
businesslike, but she'd tarried and here he was. She
watched as he walked up the drive to her front door,
his stride loose, his long legs eating up the distance.
He was hatless and the wind tousled his black hair.
He had a laptop bag tucked under his arm and his
face reflected his tension.

She couldn't see his eyes but somehow knew they
were full of frustration and irritation.

Yeah, she annoyed him as much as he did her.

She heard the intercom buzz on the lobby door
and took her time letting him in, thinking that standing in the cold might drop his temper a degree or
two. Ten seconds later, she heard the sharp rap on
her apartment door.

Tinsley opened her door and looked up, and up,
into Cody's frustrated face. "Why the hell have you
been ducking my calls?" he demanded, as he brushed
past her to step inside. He dumped his bag on the
bench and flipped open the buttons to his navy cashmere coat.

"Good morning, Cody," Tinsley replied, thinking
that one of them needed to be the adult in the room.
Then she remembered that she *had* been avoiding
him, and admitted she didn't have a leg to stand on
when it came to claiming maturity.

She took his coat, hung it up on the freestanding
coat hook and led him into her sitting room. Like

Kinga's place right next door, her bottom floor consisted of an open-plan living, dining and kitchen area. Unlike Kinga, Tinsley had kept all the redbrick walls and left the beams exposed. Her staircase to the second floor was steel rather than wood and she'd aimed for a more industrial look, replacing the wooden floors with stained concrete. The bones of the building were masculine and stark so she'd softened the room with feminine furniture, including couches covered in a fabric featuring blowsy pink, cream and red roses and bright, plain carpets.

And plants, lots and lots of indoor plants.

"Want something to drink?" Tinsley asked, hoping he wouldn't ask for coffee.

Because he was Cody and uncooperative, he did. Tinsley wrinkled her nose and waved at the coffee machine on the concrete counter. "Can you make it yourself? The smell of coffee makes me nauseous."

Cody's eyebrows shot up but he didn't say anything. He just walked into her kitchen and made himself at home. "Can I get you anything?" he asked.

She had to admit, he had good manners, Tinsley thought as she resumed her seat next to Moose. "I'm good, thanks."

A few minutes later Cody returned, carrying her favorite oversize mug. She caught the smell of coffee and her stomach lurched. She breathed deeply and, this time, nausea passed. Thank God.

Cody sat down on the chair opposite her and looked at her cat, who'd twisted himself into a furry pretzel and was taking up most of the couch. "Is that cat on steroids?" he asked.

Tinsley looked at Moose and frowned. "You'd think so but no, he's just robust."

Tinsley reached out to stroke Moose's ears and got a nip for her efforts. "You are revolting," she told him.

Looking at Cody, she shrugged. "Moose is a Maine Coon, and bigger than most."

Cody wrapped his hands around her cup, his gaze steady and cool. "Are we going to talk about cats or are we going to discuss the bombshell you dropped?"

"Cats are easy conversation," Tinsley admitted. She rubbed her fingertips across her forehead. She had a headache brewing. Along with throwing up, she had fairly constant headaches. The first trimester had been more intense than she'd imagined. She felt the familiar bubble of worry in her gut and pushed it aside. She'd visited the pregnancy sites and everyone's experience was different.

Cody put the mug on the steel-and-glass coffee table that separated them and placed his forearms on his knees. "I've been trying to reach you for days now, Tinsley."

"I didn't feel like talking to you. Or talking to anyone," she added.

Cody's eyes locked onto hers, dark and direct. "Who else knows about your pregnancy?" he demanded.

Kinga had left town the morning after the ball for a two-week trip down to Griff's Florida Keys island home, and their parents extended their stay in New York. Jules was in Palm Beach doing a pop-up bar at a new yacht club and Callum...? Well, Callum wasn't someone she'd confide in.

Besides, she wasn't ready to tell anyone. She was still trying to come to terms with this life-changing event. "No one knows but you."

Cody's glance didn't waver. "Okay. And I know you are intending to keep this baby... You haven't changed your mind?"

Tinsley rolled her eyes. "After acting like a lunatic when I heard that Heather was pregnant, I'd be a total flake if I said no now."

Cody's expression didn't change. "People are allowed to change their minds, Tinsley."

Tinsley lifted her chin. "I haven't. I won't. So, if you've come to talk me out of having this baby, then you can leave, right now."

Cody closed his eyes in frustration. "Did you always jump to conclusions or is this something new?"

She felt embarrassment heat her cheeks. "Sorry," she muttered, burying her hand in Moose's coat. She didn't like being called out—who did?—and Cody, blunt as hell, had a way of slicing through all the nonsense and homing in on the heart of the matter. Of her.

She didn't like it. At all.

Because she still wasn't ready to discuss her pregnancy, and his lack of interest in being involved, she racked her brain for a change of subject. Work was unemotional, something they could talk about without shedding each other's blood.

"Did you see the email from Callum giving us the go-ahead?" she asked.

"I did," Cody replied. "Did you notice that the figure for my remuneration was substantially reduced?"

Tinsley winced. "Sorry."

"Don't be. I inflated my original price because Callum always knocks it down. My remuneration came in fractionally over where I wanted it to be."

While Cody didn't have JT's sky-high IQ, he was damn smart. And very sneaky. "I'm sorry you have to play mind games with my grandfather," Tinsley told him.

Cody shrugged. "I'm used to it and I nearly always get what I want out of the deal."

She did not doubt that. In ten years, Cody had established an international business worth a few hundred million. He had offices and staff all over the country and internationally, he owned a stunning apartment in downtown Portland, had property in LA. He owned and occasionally flew a private jet.

He was regarded as being one of the most eligible bachelors in the country. But Tinsley wasn't interested in Cody on a long-term basis. She'd taken the Gallant name once, and was perfectly happy being a Ryder-White. It was so much less complicated.

Tinsley pulled her feet up onto her couch and sat cross-legged. "I'll be back in the office tomorrow and we can draw up a schedule, decide who's doing what."

Cody leaned back and placed his ankle on his knee. "I've issued some instructions to my staff. They are getting the ball rolling."

Uh…*no*. They couldn't do anything without her. Tinsley sat up straight and held up her hand, tasting panic at the back of her throat. How did she know what they were doing was right? Good enough? Dare she say it…perfect? "That doesn't work for me. What exactly are they doing? Why didn't you talk to me about this? I need to know what's going on!"

"Since you didn't return my calls, I got the process started. Don't call me out for doing my job when you have been unavailable!"

"I was in London," Tinsley replied, knowing it was a weak argument.

"And they don't have phones or email there?" Cody sent a contemplative look toward the ceiling. "Weird, they had those the last time I visited."

"Okay, smarty-pants, I was avoiding you," Tinsley admitted.

"I know. Don't do it again," Cody told her, his voice serious. "Apart from the fact that I needed answers from you, I was also worried about you, worried about the baby."

Nice of him to say that, but she didn't believe him for a second. Cody had made it clear that he wasn't interested in being a dad.

"Talking of…"

Oh, God, here it came. The lecture, the demands, the questions. She still wasn't ready to deal with any of it, mostly because she still somehow didn't feel pregnant—despite having done two other tests and puking every morning. Her brain was still catching up with her body.

"How are you?" Cody asked.

Tinsley looked at him, puzzled by his question. "Sorry?"

"I'm not speaking Farsi, Tinsley. I want to know how you are."

Oh. Um…right. She didn't have the energy to lie. "Constantly tired, and best friends with the toilet bowl."

Cody winced. "Still?"

"According to the literature, it should stop sometime between twelve and sixteen weeks but, in extreme cases, it can last the entire pregnancy." God, she hoped that didn't happen to her.

"Have you seen a doctor yet?" Cody asked her. He sounded so calm, she thought, unfazed.

"I called my ob-gyn, and she said that, because I'm young and healthy, I just need to carry on as normal, though she did give me some vitamins. She wants to see me when I'm twelve weeks along, for an ultrasound."

"And that will tell us what?"

He'd said *us*, not *you* and Tinsley wondered why that caused excitement to race along her nerve endings. *He's just your sperm donor, Ryder-White, not*

Treat Yourself with 2 Free Books!

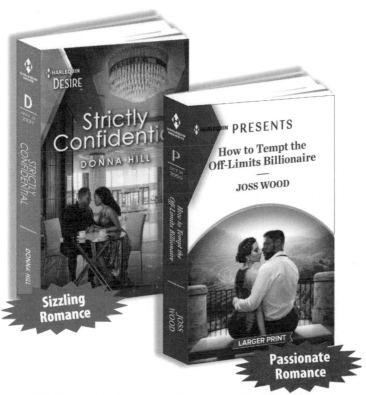

Sizzling Romance

Passionate Romance

GET UP TO 4 FREE BOOKS & 2 FREE GIFTS WORTH OVER $20

See Inside For Details

Claim Them While You Can

Get ready to relax and indulge with your **FREE BOOKS** and more!

Claim up to FOUR NEW BOOKS & TWO MYSTERY GIFTS – absolutely FREE!

Dear Reader,

We both know life can be difficult at times. That's why it's important to treat yourself so you can relax and recharge once in a while.

And I'd like to help you do this by sending you this amazing offer of up to FOUR brand new full length FREE BOOKS that WE pay for.

This is everything I have ready to send to you right now:

Try **Harlequin® Desire** books featuring the worlds of the American elite with juicy plot twists, delicious sensuality and intriguing scandal.

Try **Harlequin Presents® Larger-Print** books featuring the glamorous lives of royals and billionaires in a world of exotic locations, where passion knows no bounds.

Or **TRY BOTH!**

All we ask in return is that you answer 4 simple questions on the attached Treat Yourself survey. You'll get **Two Free Books** and **Two Mystery Gifts** from each series you try, *altogether worth over $20!* Who could pass up a deal like that?

Sincerely,

Pam Powers

Harlequin Reader Service

Treat Yourself to Free Books and Free Gifts.

Answer 4 fun questions and get rewarded.

▼ DETACH AND MAIL CARD TODAY! ▼

	YES	NO
1. I LOVE reading a good book.	○	○
2. I indulge and "treat" myself often.	○	○
3. I love getting FREE things.	○	○
4. Reading is one of my favorite activities.	○	○

TREAT YOURSELF • Pick your 2 Free Books...

Yes! Please send me my Free Books from each series I select and Free Mystery Gifts. I understand that I am under no obligation to buy anything, as explained on the back of this card.

Which do you prefer?

❑ **Harlequin Desire®** 225/326 HDL GRAN
❑ **Harlequin Presents® Larger-Print** 176/376 HDL GRAN
❑ **Try Both** 225/326 & 176/376 HDL GRAY

FIRST NAME   LAST NAME

ADDRESS

APT.#   CITY

STATE/PROV.   ZIP/POSTAL CODE

EMAIL ❑   Please check this box if you would like to receive newsletters and promotional emails from Harlequin Enterprises ULC and its affiliates. You can unsubscribe anytime.

HD/HP-520-TY22

▲ If offer card is missing write to: Harlequin Reader Service, P.O. Box 1341, Buffalo, NY 14240-8531 or visit www.ReaderService.com ▲

BUSINESS REPLY MAIL
FIRST-CLASS MAIL PERMIT NO. 717 BUFFALO, NY

POSTAGE WILL BE PAID BY ADDRESSEE

HARLEQUIN READER SERVICE
PO BOX 1341
BUFFALO NY 14240-8571

NO POSTAGE
NECESSARY
IF MAILED
IN THE
UNITED STATES

*your baby's daddy or your happy-ever-after. You
don't believe in those, remember?*

"That scan, the twelve-week one, accurately de-
termines my due date, whether I'm having twins,
or more—"

Cody scraped a hand over his face. "Jesus."

She smiled as color leached from his face. Though
why he was looking gray, she had no idea; she would
be the one doing everything. "The scan also checks
whether everything is okay with the baby, and they
also do some sort of screening test—I can't remember its name—for conditions like Down syndrome."

Cody's piercing look pinned her to the chair. "And
if there is something wrong with the baby, what will
you do?"

Tinsley laid a hand on her heart and jerked her
shoulders up. "I don't know, Cody. I'm not thinking
about that! I'm not going into what-ifs, not now, I *can't*."

Cody picked up his coffee mug and downed the
contents. Tinsley winced, thinking it must be ice-
cold by now. He put the cup down and sent her a
brooding look, but didn't speak again. Deciding to
address the elephant in the room, she dropped her
feet to the floor and echoed his pose, her arms on
her thighs. "Cody, this isn't your problem. I told you
that I am happy to have this baby on my own, without any input from you. But—"

One dark eyebrow raised.

"But I do need you to believe that I didn't plan on
this happening. I would never trick a man into being

a dad. That's too big a decision to force on someone else." Because he was so very direct, she thought she could be too. After all, if he was going to dish it, he should be able to take it.

"Part of the reason I was ignoring you is that I'm still hugely pissed off that you thought I would do that."

Shame and regret flashed in his eyes as he pushed a hand through his hair. "Yeah, I should apologize for that. I was upset, a little freaked out."

Tinsley waited. And then waited some more. But no apology came. "You suck at apologies, Gallant," she muttered.

A small smile touched his lips. "I do." He glanced down at his hands before looking up at her again. He hauled in some air. "I am sorry, Tinsley. I was out of line."

"Accepted." Tinsley rested her elbows on her knees and speared her hands through her hair.

"We need to talk about my involvement in this process, Tinsley."

Tinsley handed him a sharp look. "How involved do you want to be?"

Cody winced, then took a moment to think. "A part of me wants to let you do this on your own, then I think that I'm a goddamn coward. Another part of me knows I have to, at the very least, pay you for child support, which won't be a problem, *ever*. Another part of me, admittedly still an exceedingly small slice, could be excited. I don't know what to think or how to feel!"

And for someone like Cody, who was so decisive, that uncertainty had to be upsetting. "I don't need an answer today, Cody. Or even tomorrow."

"Thank God. Because I don't have one today and won't have one tomorrow," Cody muttered.

He was trying to wrap his head around this, just as she was. Having a kid was a damn big deal and it was a lot to think about. But they still had time, over seven months to be more precise; nothing needed to be decided now.

So much could happen between now and then, and she didn't wear rose-colored glasses. "Cody, as much as I want this kid, I am trying to be realistic. According to Dr. Internet, between fifteen and twenty percent of pregnancies cnd in miscarriage, but they think that figure could be higher. Those miscarriages usually happen in the first trimester."

Cody gestured for her to carry on talking.

"It's still so early in the process so I would suggest that we take this step by step, day by day," Tinsley said. "We should try and get along, not only because of this—" she pointed to her stomach "—but also because we're going to be working together."

Cody's nod came slowly but it was there. "Okay, we can try that. What else?"

"I'd like to keep this between us, for now. Nobody needs to know yet."

"You don't want to rub it in JT's face?"

She had; she couldn't deny it. A part of her wanted to send a generic email, telling him that she was also having a baby, *with his brother*. Then she realized that was just her inner mean girl talking. "No, JT doesn't matter."

"Your breath hitched when you said his name," Cody stated, his tone harsher than before. "Are you still in love with him, Tinsley?"

Tinsley stood up and walked over to the window and stood next to a two-drawer credenza. In the left-hand drawer was a photograph in a silver frame, face-down. It was her favorite picture of her and JT, taken in Hawaii, while they were on their honeymoon.

JT sat on a lounger reading a book, and she was curled up in his lap. She was looking up at him, love in her eyes, adoration on her face. His full attention was on his book. From that moment on, for the rest of their marriage, Tinsley had to fight for his attention.

Yet she'd been so convinced that they'd had a happy marriage and his request for a divorce devastated her. In hindsight, she knew that she had looked at her marriage and seen what she wanted to see, not what it was…

She'd never do that again.

She looked out the window and watched the fat flakes of snow drifting to the ground. "No, I don't love him—I did but I don't. Not anymore."

From across the room, she heard Cody's sigh, heard the slap of his hands against his knees. In the reflection of the window, she saw him move toward her, his hands coming to rest on her shoulders. He bent his head to speak in her ear, his breath warm on her cheek. "Good," he murmured. "That makes life a lot easier and I won't feel weird for wanting to kiss you."

Tinsley tipped her head back to look at him. "And are you planning on kissing me?" she asked, her voice a little breathless.

"That would be a hell-to-the-yes," Cody murmured, covering her mouth with his.

Cody slowly turned her and placed his hands on her hips, his mouth, surprisingly tender, moving over hers. He kissed her like he was unwrapping a much-anticipated present on Christmas Day, drawing out the moment, making it last. A nibble here, a gentle suck there, a brush of his tongue against hers.

Tinsley lifted her hand to his jaw, felt the scratch of his three-day-old beard, rough against her hand. She skimmed her hand down his neck and slid her fingers under the open collar of his shirt, looking for the heat of his skin. He was so big, so masculine, and he made her feel precious and petite. She was an alpha boss girl, content to walk her own path, independent as hell, but there was something amazing about standing in a powerful man's arms.

And the fact that Cody Gallant desired her—which was fairly obvious—made her feel intensely feminine and imbued with a power of her own. Feeling his arms pulling her closer, she sighed when he deepened the kiss, his hand on the back of her head changing the angle. Tender turned to tempestuous as he cupped her ass with his big hand, the other dropping to slide under the back of her jersey, tracing the knobs of her spine.

Reality disappeared and there was only the two of them, exchanging deep kisses as fat snowflakes drifted down beyond the windowpane. Needing to get closer, she pulled his shirt out of his pants and slid her hand over his skin, her fingers dancing across the ridges of his stomach. He was so warm, so solid, so incredibly skilled at raising her core temperature to sweltering. The urge to strip him was strong.

She couldn't help the words that slipped off her tongue. "Come upstairs with me."

Cody tensed, pulled his mouth off hers and released a low groan. Moving his hands to her hips, he pulled in a couple of ragged breaths before stepping back. He raked his fingers through his already tousled hair and tipped his head back to look at the ceiling.

So, that would be a *no* then.

Embarrassed at her lack of control—what was it about this man that caused her brain to shut down?— Tinsley whipped around, conscious of her bloodred cheeks and knowing her neck would also be blotchy. She wasn't used to propositioning men; she'd probably done it wrong. Too blunt, too in your face...

But she thought that men—Cody especially because he was so damn direct—liked up-front and honest. But what the hell did she know?

She forced herself to turn around, to look at him, and when she did, she frowned, surprised. Cody stared out the window, his hands in his pockets, thoughtful surprise on his face and in his eyes. And a healthy dose of confusion...

He sighed before his eyes met hers. "I didn't come here to take you to bed, Tins. Don't get me wrong, I want to because taking you to bed is all I've thought about lately. But I think sex is a complication neither of us needs right now."

She stared at him, trying to parse his words, to find the hidden meaning. Then she remembered that he wasn't like his brother, who liked playing mind games. Cody said what he meant. And when she thought about it, sleeping together was a complication neither of them needed. They were work colleagues and they both still needed to wrap their heads around her pregnancy. She was still processing the news, working through her emotions.

It was so easy to daydream but reality had dumped a cold bucket of water on those rosy fantasies.

Really, what did she know about being a mommy? It was all very well to say that she was financially and emotionally ready, but was she? She was going to be doing it alone...

That wasn't what she'd planned. Though, honestly, if she'd had a baby with JT, that was probably what would've happened. He'd barely participated in their marriage, so she doubted that he'd have shown any interest in their child.

And people wondered why she was a control freak; it was because she had to be. In her quest for a perfect marriage and to be a perfect wife, she'd paid their bills and booked their holidays, arranged for car services and annual checkups. She balanced checkbooks and planned meals. Sometimes, most times toward the end, she'd felt like JT's nanny, not his wife.

Cody came to stand next to her and briefly, gently squeezed her shoulder. "We need to work together and you're pregnant. I think we have enough on our plate, don't you?"

He was right, so Tinsley nodded. Folding her arms across her chest, she tipped her head to the side. "I agree. So, work. Where are we and what do we need to do?"

"Everything," Cody stated. He glanced at his watch before sitting down on the sofa and picking up his laptop bag to pull out a state-of-the-art, streamlined laptop. "I have a few hours before I need to take a meeting back at the office, so let's strategize."

She could strategize, Tinsley thought, walking over to her desk and picking up her trusty iPad. She sat down opposite him, tucked her feet under her butt and rested her tablet on her knee. She'd far prefer to go back to sleep—or for her and Cody to go upstairs for some naked fun—but she could work.

She had to; in seven or so months she'd have an additional mouth to feed.

Babies, she'd heard, weren't cheap.

Seven

A few hours later, Cody looked at Tinsley, tucked into her chair, black-framed glasses on her pretty nose. Her fingers raced across her tablet's small keyboard, and noticing that she was in the zone, he decided he needed more coffee. She didn't notice when he stood up and headed for her kitchen.

It was snowing hard outside, and the wind had picked up. Wonderful. He couldn't wait for winter to be over. He wanted the heat of summer, to feel the sun on his skin. If he wasn't so swamped, he'd head down to the Caribbean and dive in those warm waters, doze in the sun and sleep with his windows and doors wide open, cooled by island breezes.

But he had too much to do here, too many responsibilities. And he'd gathered one more: Tinsley and her baby. His baby. *Theirs*.

Cody glared at the coffee machine. He'd spent the past week digesting the news, trying to make sense of the turn his life had taken. Initially, he'd wanted to be angry, but spending New Year's Eve together had been a choice they'd *both* made. While he'd used a condom, he knew that abstinence was the only foolproof means of contraception. Abstinence had never been an option—he liked sex, dammit—so he'd taken his chances, rolled the dice and for twenty years or so he'd won against the house. This one time, with his ex-sister-in-law, he'd lost.

She'd all but given him permission to walk away, to be an anonymous sperm donor. She'd told him she was happy to be a single mom and yeah, he'd be lying if he said he wasn't initially, briefly tempted to walk away. After raising JT, being responsible for his brother's welfare at such a young age, he'd vowed never to put himself in the position of looking after anyone but himself again.

He looked at Tinsley again, taking in her thin face and tired eyes. The pregnancy was hard on her, anyone could see that, but he admired her just-push-through-it attitude.

She was a strong woman and he admired strength, tenacity, the ability to keep on carrying on.

In some ways, they were very alike. Driven, determined, stoic. They both demanded too much, liked getting their way.

And, despite the big complication of the pregnancy and having to work together, he was still insanely attracted to her, to this woman who made him feel scratchy, off-balance and out of sorts. Since New Year's Eve, he just had to think of her and his heart sped up and his lungs forgot how to do their job. He recalled, in Technicolor detail, every kiss, the silkiness of her skin, her breathy voice in his ear telling him how good he made her feel.

And when he was with her, he couldn't keep himself from touching her, partly from desire, but also because in his arms was where he needed her to be. In his arms, she could relax, and she could rest. Tinsley raised his protective instincts and he couldn't work out why.

Because of all the professional women he knew, she was the one who seemed to have all her shit together, all the time. She was smart, organized, incredibly efficient. She did the work of five men and juggled a hundred balls in the air. He knew that if there was anyone who could rock being a single mom, Tinsley would be that woman.

But sometimes Cody sensed that buried beneath her self-sufficient attitude was someone not as tough as she portrayed herself to be. He knew his brother, knew that JT expected everything done for him all the time. Cody had no doubt Tinsley had done all the heavy lifting in their marriage. Taking charge was probably a habit for her but suspected she wouldn't mind someone to occasionally relieve her of the responsibilities she carried around with deceptive ease.

When she thought he wasn't looking, she sometimes looked a little lost, like she was desperate for someone to throw her a lifeline.

But Cody was always honest with himself, and he knew that could be his ego talking, his need to protect rising like a tide.

After his mom died and his father checked out, he'd taken on the responsibility of raising JT. At twelve he was planning their meals, juggling their schedules, and getting JT to school on time. His father employed a housekeeper to oversee the two boys but Cody had taken control and by the time he was fifteen, Mrs. K answered to him and not the other way around.

Until the day JT met Tinsley. Only months into their relationship, Tinsley had JT firmly in hand. She reminded him to eat, to get a haircut, took him clothes shopping. Within a year, she had the codes to his bank cards and swiftly became best friends with their housekeeper.

JT and Tinsley left for college in Boston and moved into an off-campus apartment together and Cody took advantage of his freedom. He partied hard, slept around and vowed that he'd never again take on the responsibility of another person.

But now Tinsley was having his baby, which made him rethink everything. And, for some absurd reason, he wanted to make life easier for her. She hadn't had an easy life with his brother—JT was a difficult guy.

Cody was still pissed at JT for treating Tinsley like trash. Cody wasn't a forever type of guy, but he figured that when and if a man did jump into a relationship, he should stick to his guns, keep his word and do everything he could to make it work. JT had promised to love, honor and cherish Tinsley, but when he was sick of her and sick of their marriage , he swiftly moved on.

"So, a couple of days ago I sent an email to a TV show producer I know, someone who regularly produces shows for the Food Network," Tinsley said, lifting her voice so that it carried over to him. "I pitched the idea of a documentary about the cocktail competition, and he's interested. He wants to know if we can fly out for a meeting this weekend."

Coffee forgotten, Cody walked back into the living room, sincerely surprised. "Seriously?"

Tinsley lifted one shoulder, her eyes sparkling with excitement. "I thought it was a long shot, but he sounded excited." She placed a hand on her heart. "Frankly, I'm stunned."

He was too. "Where is he based?"

"In LA, but he's at his house in Avalon. That's on—"

"Catalina Island," Cody finished her sentence. He knew the town, had dived its waters and had taken summer vacations there. "I know it."

"He can spare us a few hours on Sunday afternoon to do a pitch," Tinsley told him. "I've emailed him to tell him we'll be there."

Cody stared at her, taking a moment to digest her words and to push down his rising frustration. "Tinsley, I have a brunch meeting in New York on Sunday morning, one that I can't blow off."

Tinsley dared to wink. "Blow her off, Cody. This is important."

Look, he knew he had a rep for bouncing from woman to woman—and it was exaggerated, mostly predicated on his behavior in his midtwenties—but he hadn't slept with anyone since her. And hadn't wanted to...

Beside the point.

"You're jumping to conclusions, Tinsley," Cody told her, his voice rock-hard. "One of the reasons I've been looking for you is to tell you that I secured a meeting with Geraint du Pont, and he's interested in judging the competition."

Tinsley's eyes widened. "Holy crap, that's amazing. As well as being one of the best chefs in the country, he's young, gorgeous and charismatic."

"He just sold his restaurant in New York and is looking for a new venture, so he has the time. But he's flying to London on Sunday afternoon, so Sunday morning is the only time he can see us," Cody told her, gripping the back of the sofa.

"Why didn't you tell me?" Tinsley demanded, temper flaring in her eyes.

"I did say, in one of the many emails you didn't answer, that I have a line on an exciting judge and to please call me urgently. But because you were ignoring me, or punishing me or something, here we are, double-booked," Cody snapped. "Why didn't you check with me before you agreed to the Catalina Island meeting?"

"Because I knew this was an opportunity we couldn't pass on!" Tinsley retorted.

"Neither is getting Geraint du Pont for a judge!"

They stared at each other; their gazes hot, equally annoyed. Cody broke their standoff. "You can't make decisions for me, Tinsley. That's unacceptable."

"Hey, you also made an arrangement I didn't agree to!"

"At least I tried to talk to you about it, and you know it!"

Embarrassment flashed in her eyes as she stood up. But her posture and expression turned defiant. "I'll go to Catalina Island. You talk to Geraint du Pont. Sorted," Tinsley said, her tone flippant.

Not by a long shot. He needed her to realize that they were a team, that she wasn't doing this alone. "You need to work on your communication skills, Tinsley. Also, this might be a Ryder project and you might be my client, but I don't work for you."

"Look, if you aren't happy with the way I work, then pull out. I'll get this project done. I always do."

She'd like that because then she would have complete control. But she'd also be working under maximum stress. "Even if I agreed to that, and I never would, have you forgotten that you're pregnant, that you spend a lot of time throwing up and that working fourteen- or sixteen-hour days right now might not be good for the baby?"

She opened her mouth to argue, backed down and pursed her lips. Taking advantage of the break in the conversation, he plowed on. "We're a goddamn team, Tinsley," he stated, glancing at her stomach, "in more ways than at work. That means we have to talk, and neither of us gets to make unilateral decisions anymore. Can you do that?"

"Can you?" Tinsley countered.

"Yeah, I can."

Tinsley pushed her hands into her hair, dislodging several strands. Her mouth moved and he was fairly sure she muttered an under-her-breath curse word. She looked up at the ceiling, out the window, at her cat—anywhere but at him.

"I'm not good at delegating, Cody," she finally admitted. He admired her honesty.

He fought his urge to run his hand over her hair, to comfort and soothe. Reassuring her now would lead to greater problems down the line. "Well, learn. And learn quickly," he said, deliberately abrupt.

She glared at the command in his voice, not at all happy with his authoritarian tone. That was fine; he wasn't particularly happy with her either.

He glanced at his watch, and thanks to the decreasing visibility due to the snow, realized that he was probably going to be late for his next meeting. "I don't have time to argue with you. I need to get back to the office."

"So you can give your staff more instructions about our event? That's pretty hypocritical, Gallant."

Cody counted to ten, to twenty. "Again, if you bothered to read all my emails, you'd know that I gave my art department leeway to work on a logo for the competition, subject to discussion. I also asked my PR person to draw up a couple of press releases, also subject to discussion." He narrowed his eyes at her, wondering how he could still want to kiss her, take her to bed, when irritation rocked inside him. "Did you hear those words, Ryder? 'Subject to discussion' means you and I will *talk* about it. About everything."

"I get it," Tinsley muttered, unable to hold his eyes.

He picked up his laptop, shoved it into its bag and walked over to the hallway and yanked his jacket off the hook, pulling it on with practiced ease. "You go to Catalina Island. I'll meet with du Pont," he snapped the words out. "But let's make this the last time we act independently, Tinsley."

Tinsley lifted her hand to her forehead in a sharp salute and clicked her feet together. "Sir, yes sir!"

"Smart-ass," Cody grumbled, yanking open her front door and wincing at the cold. This woman was going to cause him countless hours of lost sleep.

And if they had a daughter, he had no doubt she'd do the same. God help him.

The following Sunday, Cody braced himself as he stepped from his lounge onto the balcony of his apartment and cursed as a breeze blew off the water and plastered his Henley and comfortable track pants to his body. Gripping the railing, he took in his awesome view of the waterfront and cityscape, the roads and rooftops covered with snow. The sun would drop soon and, with it, the temperature. But at least the roads were clear, for now.

Another massive storm was due to hit the city in the next few hours. He hoped Tinsley made it home before she had to drive in the blizzard. Cody rubbed his arms and told himself to stop worrying, Tinsley had been driving in bad weather since she was a kid, so she was no more likely to have an accident than he was. Unless she was tired, still feeling nauseous and unable to concentrate...

He kept asking her how she was, and she kept ducking the question. Along with dinner tonight, they were also going to have a conversation about her going to the doctor to get checked out. They'd met several times this week and, through her expertly applied makeup, he noticed the green pallor to her skin, the dark rings under her eyes and the perpetual squint that suggested a constant headache.

Weren't pregnant women supposed to glow?

They'd agreed to meet at his apartment tonight after they both flew in to debrief and he'd told her that he'd bring pizza from his favorite place in Queens. The two massive pies were sitting on the island in his kitchen, along with a bottle of red for him and her imported ginger beer. It helped with the nausea, or so she'd informed him, and she drank the stuff by the gallon. He'd read the nutrition labels and saw that it was filled with sugar, but Tinsley hadn't picked up any weight. If anything she'd dropped a pound or two.

There had to be something the doctors could do for her...

Cody took in a couple of breaths, the air cactus-spiky as it slid down his throat. Clouds were moving in, and the storm was fast approaching. He glanced at his watch; Tinsley was cutting it close.

She'd be fine...

Cody glared at the sky and walked back inside. He loved his luxurious, five thousand square feet of brilliantly designed space. His apartment had high ceilings, loads of natural light and amazing architectural accents. The modern kitchen opened to the dining area and a fabulous living room, dominated by a large fireplace. The floor-to-ceiling doors could be opened onto the expansive balcony, a place where he could entertain effortlessly and frequently. He had a huge master suite, three other bedrooms and a home study.

Best of all, it was just a few minutes' walk from his downtown Portland offices and, even in the dead of winter, he often walked the short distance to work. If he needed a car during the day, he could either pick up one of his company vehicles or jog back to his place to pick up his Mercedes SUV or, if he was feeling brave, the exceptionally rare and valuable 1963 Ferrari 250 GTO he'd picked up in a rare car auction five years ago.

Picking up his phone, he dialed Tinsley's number. She answered after a couple of heart-stopping rings. "How far are you?" he demanded.

"Pulling into your place right now," she replied. "The roads were empty, surprisingly, with no accidents."

Brilliant news, Cody thought. He rubbed his chest

above his heart as he told her where to park. As the owner of the penthouse, and the building, he had an additional two undercover parking spaces close to his personal elevator. Jabbing a button on his tablet, he sent the lift down to the parking garage. He tossed the tablet onto a soft cushion on the couch and pushed his fingers into his hair. She was here, and she was safe.

And his baby was safe.

That was all that mattered.

His baby?

Cody gripped the back of his couch and dropped his head between his outstretched arms. Yeah, that sounded right. His baby. The one he'd never thought he wanted. Somehow, over the past week, the idea of having a child had stopped scaring him and started to excite him. He wanted to know more, know *everything*. He wanted to be involved. He'd never half assed anything in his life and he didn't intend to start now. Cody straightened. He and Tinsley were going to have some exceedingly long conversations over the next few months…

He heard a rap on his front door and then the door pushed open, and he saw her white face. He strode over to her and opened the door wider, gesturing for her to enter. When she did, she swayed on her feet and the little color she had drained from her face.

He grabbed her, lowered her to the ground and helped her put her head between her knees. "I hope you only felt light-headed once you parked, Ryder-

White, because if you drove like this, I'm going to lose my shit," he told her.

She lifted her head and looked at him with purple-blue eyes. "No, I was fine, I promise. I only started feeling dizzy when I got out of the car."

"Follow-up question…so why didn't you call me and ask me to come down and help you?"

Tinsley rested her head against the wall as a smidgen of color reentered her face. Her mouth tightened and that all-too-familiar light of battle appeared in her eyes. Then she sighed and a hint of amusement touched her lips. "Because I'm ridiculously stubborn and chronically independent?"

Cody clicked his fingers and pointed his index finger at her. Standing up, he held out his hand. "Are you feeling better? Can you stand up?"

Tinsley slid her much smaller hand into his and he pulled her up, thinking that she was as light as a feather. When she pulled her hands from his, he watched with narrowed eyes to see whether she'd wobble and when she didn't, he bent down to pick up her heavy tote bag as she slid out of her cashmere coat.

He led her across the room and gestured for her to sit down on the corner sofa seat, the one closest to his wood-burning fireplace. The room was darker than before, the clouds blocking out the last of the light, and he flipped on a lamp. "Need anything?" he asked. "I have tea, various types—all of which taste disgusting by the way—soft drinks, that ginger beer you like."

"I'd really like tea, chamomile if you have it," she looked around his place, obviously impressed. "And I'd love a tour of your place. It looks fabulous."

"Sure, but later."

Tinsley bent down and removed her brown leather flat-soled knee-high boots, placing them to the side of the couch. She wore a thigh-length fisherman's sweater over tight jeans and under a blue, puffy vest. A voluminous scarf, in shades of green and blue, was wrapped around her neck. She pulled off the scarf, then the vest and placed them in a neat pile next to her boots. She gestured to her feet. "Do you mind if I pull my feet up on your furniture?"

"Go for it," he told her. " I'll go and make you that tea."

When he returned, just five minutes later, her head was on a pillow resting on the arm of his couch, she was stretched out and was deeply asleep. Smiling, Cody went to the hallway closet, pulled a soft, light blanket off the shelf and draped it over her slim frame.

And outside, the storm gathered in intensity. The wind shook the windows and fat, huge snowballs smacked his overlarge windows. She'd made it, with no time to spare, and he was profoundly grateful that she was safe with him and not out there trying to drive through the raging, wicked storm.

Eight

Tinsley shot up, disoriented. She was in a strange, but lovely sitting room. Across from her were tall, wide windows. The darkness beyond them was broken by white dots of falling snow. Pushing back her hair, she sat up slowly, and looked around, her eyes landing on Cody, sitting across from her, working on a laptop.

"Hi," she murmured, sounding like she was half-asleep.

Cody lifted his head and smiled. "Hey."

"How long did I sleep?" Tinsley asked as she sat up, pushing her hair off her face.

Cody consulted his expensive watch. "Three and a half hours."

Tinsley pulled a face. "Why didn't you wake me

up?" she demanded. "I need to get home, feed Moose."

Cody closed his laptop and moved it to the occasional table next to him. "I called Kinga. She said she would feed Moose. And she doesn't want you driving home tonight. I agree."

It really annoyed her when people tried to tell her what to do. She was a responsible adult, dammit, and she'd been making her own decisions for a while now. She stood up, walked over to the window and scowled at the whirling snow.

"They're predicting whiteout conditions for the rest of the night and possibly tomorrow."

Cody's words sank in and her stomach dropped. "I'm stuck here for the foreseeable future?"

Cody nodded as he stood up. "Looks like it."

Tinsley cursed softly, partly at the idea of not being home, with her cat, partly because she was more excited than she should be at the thought of staying with Cody. Proximity wasn't a good idea. She was far too aware of Cody. She spent too much time thinking about making love with him again, remembering what he felt like, his gorgeous smell, his drugging kisses.

She wanted that again. She wanted to lose herself in his touch, slide away on pleasure, pretend that nothing existed outside his soul-stealing touch.

But she'd had him once, or he'd had her; all that remained were the memories of an awesome night. They had complicated family ties, business pressures and a baby on the way. Losing themselves in each other again was an impossibility.

"Are you hungry?" Cody asked from somewhere behind her.

She pulled her eyes off the snow and onto his reflection in the glass. He stood next to his chair, arms folded, his expression unreadable. In his supercasual clothes and with messy hair and thick stubble, he looked a little rough and a lot hot.

Then her stomach rumbled, pulling her thoughts out of the bedroom and into the kitchen. "Starving, actually. What's on the menu?" she asked as she turned around.

"Pepperoni pizza, or, if your stomach can't handle that, plain cheese."

"Frozen?" Tinsley asked, unable to stop her nose from wrinkling. She wasn't a fan—she was a pizza snob and if she couldn't get it from her favorite places, she'd make her own, from scratch—but if frozen was all that was on offer, she'd take it.

Cody walked into the open-plan kitchen and lifted two boxes with their distinctive red, white and green geometric pattern. Now they were talking!

"You have pizza from Lombardi's?"

Cody raised his eyebrows. "You know it?"

"I love it! Griff brought pizza back from New York for Kinga and when I heard about it, I was so annoyed that I didn't get a late-night invitation to join them."

"Judging by the way those two carry on, I think

you would've been a very obvious third wheel," Cody said, as he pulled out plates from a cabinet. "And let's be honest here—you don't share your pizza with just anyone."

"But you'll share yours with me?" Tinsley asked, resting her forearms on the white granite counter of the island.

"Thinking about it," Cody teased. "But if you prefer girl food, there might be some yogurt in the fridge and granola in the cupboard."

Tinsley slapped her hand on the closest pizza box and mock growled. "Do not make me hurt you, Gallant."

Cody laughed. "You're about as intimidating as a pink, fluffy unicorn, Tinsley." He popped the pizza boxes in the eye-level oven to warm them. Turning to the fridge, he pulled out a bottle of her preferred brand of ginger beer—sweet of him to stock some for her—and lifted it in a silent question. When she nodded, he poured the liquid into a glass before pouring himself a glass of red wine.

Cody took a sip of his wine before lowering his glass. "I'm presuming that you're still abstaining from alcohol?"

"You presume right. It's not good for the baby and the smell makes me want to gag."

Cody rubbed his lower jaw. "When are you seeing your doctor, Tins?"

She'd been slammed at work and forgotten to

make the appointment. "I'm eight weeks now, so sometime in the next month."

"Look, I don't know a lot about kids but I've never heard of anyone being so sick from being pregnant. Maybe you should see her this week."

Ah, her doctor was one of the best on the East Coast and the chance of getting a quick appointment wasn't in the cards. If she said it was an emergency, Dr. Higgs would make a plan for her, but otherwise, she just had to grin and bear it, as she told Cody.

"Then just see a family practitioner," Cody suggested.

"I want to wait for Dr. Higgs. She's a great doctor and I can do the ultrasound and everything else while I'm there," Tinsley told him. She wasn't a doctor snob, she had the utmost respect for general practitioners, but she felt—strangely and strongly—that she needed to see a specialist.

"I wonder how Heather is feeling," Tinsley mused and when Cody's head shot up and his eyes slammed into hers, she wished she'd kept the words behind her teeth.

"Is this a competition?" he demanded.

"No, of course not," she told him. "But I can't deny that a part of me, the part I name Ms. Complete Bitch, is hoping she's puking her guts out."

"You're still angry...at him, at them," he commented.

Tinsley opened her mouth to issue a denial but

snapped her jaw closed at the last minute. Was she still angry? Yes. And no.

"I'm angry that I wasted so much time on him, that I did so much and he did so little. JT was so passive-aggressive, Cody, I never knew whether I was in his good books or bad." She looked down at her ring finger, bare now. "I would've done anything for him, and pretty much did. The only thing I asked for was a baby."

She scrunched up her face. "Heather moved in six months after we separated, married him a week after our divorce came through and now's she pregnant. I moved heaven and earth to make him happy, to create an amazing life for us and I'm pissed about that."

Cody's only response was a lift of his eyebrows and a quick nod. He turned to open the oven door and removed the pizza boxes from the oven. Picking them up he nodded to the plates. "If you could grab those, that would be good."

Tinsley did as he asked and followed him back into the living room, sinking to the floor on one side of his coffee table. Cody placed the boxes on the table and returned to the kitchen to fetch his glass of wine. When he returned, he sat down opposite Tinsley and nudged a box toward her.

After munching through one slice, Cody picked up another and held it in his hand, looking contemplative. "Talking about the past, I think we need to dig into why you and I have always had a contentious relationship."

Damn, just when she was feeling reasonably re-laxed. Tinsley carefully laid her half-eaten slice on a plate and wiped her mouth with a napkin. "Why? My marriage is over, so rehashing the fact that you never supported us is a moot point."

Hearing her sharp tone, she winced. She picked up her slice, took a small bite and stared at the melty, gooey cheese.

Cody took a long time to speak again. "You're right I didn't support you. I always believed your marriage was a mistake. And it turned out I was right."

Tinsley tossed her slice down and placed her arms on the table. "I suppose you cracked open a bottle of champagne and celebrated me being out of JT's life," she muttered.

"No, don't stop eating," Cody commanded her. "And of course I didn't. I could never celebrate something I knew caused you pain, Tins."

To his credit, he sounded frustrated. "Do I believe that you are both better off? Yes. Did I ever want to see you hurt? No, I didn't. Believe it or not, I've al-ways liked you…"

"But I was never good enough for your brother…" Tinsley replied, bitter. Why were they even discuss-ing this? Her marriage was over and JT had moved on. She had too.

"Is that what you think?" Cody demanded, look-ing surprised. "That's such a load of crap. I never, not once, thought you weren't good enough for JT."

"Then what was the problem?" Tinsley demanded, leaning forward. She wanted to eat her pizza in peace and enjoy the crackle of the fire and Cody's company. She didn't want to discuss her marriage anymore.

"You sorta hinted at it earlier. JT never loved you half as much as you loved him. If he ever loved you at all."

Tinsley wanted to bat his words away, to shove them back into their box and slam the lid closed. His words stung. It was said that, in any relationship, one person loved the other more, but she knew that JT hadn't loved her a fraction of the amount she'd loved him. It was her love, attention, commitment and effort that carried and sustained their relationship for so long.

She felt like a complete fool for giving so much and taking so little.

Cody wolfed down another slice, leaned back and turned his legs away from the table. He crossed his ankles and rested his linked hands on his stomach. "Let me get this out and, hopefully, we can put this behind us and move on."

Tinsley held her breath, not sure if she was ready to hear his opinion on her defunct marriage. No, she definitely didn't want to hear it, but she knew that the air between them needed to be cleared.

"JT has a very big brain, he's an intellectual giant but he knows nothing when it comes to interpersonal relationships…" Cody said, his eyes not leaving hers.

"He was a huge nerd and when the prettiest girl in school, smart and popular too, started paying attention to him, he enjoyed the prestige that came with being your boyfriend. But, because he's lazy, he gave as little of himself as he could get away with."

All true, Tinsley conceded.

"He neglected you, Tinsley—it's what he does." Cody rubbed the back of his neck. "This might come as a surprise to you, but I've always been more worried about you than him."

"But…he's your *brother*! You've been looking after him since your mom died!"

Cody nodded. "And I know him better than anybody, including—dare I say it?—you." He shrugged. "Jonathan Thomas is a cerebral guy, and, unlike you, isn't someone who needs love. He's a leech. He takes and takes."

Tinsley silently agreed. JT defined emotional unavailability. "Intimacy and responsibility scare him," Cody added.

"Maybe he's changed. He sounded so happy about being a father, about having a baby," Tinsley pointed out.

"Because he knows that is what is expected of him. Give him a couple of months, and a few hundred sleepless nights, and the novelty will wear off."

God, he was so right.

"I remember the night before your wedding so clearly. You were wearing your dress and the designer was in a flap because you'd lost weight, the dress didn't fit you properly and she needed to make some last-minute alterations."

Tinsley's mouth fell open. She'd forgotten about that. "She was so mad."

"You always lose weight when you're stressed," Cody told her. "And in the months leading up to your wedding you were as stressed as I've ever seen you." He frowned at her. "Well, up until now."

"I was determined to be the perfect bride," Tinsley told him. "And to start our married life with a perfect wedding."

"And I bet JT was less than interested." Cody scratched his forehead when she nodded. "By the way, you are far too obsessed with perfection."

Yeah, they definitely weren't going there. "Why did you ask me not to marry him?" Tinsley asked.

"Well, I was trying to protect you more than I was him," Cody admitted. "I spoke to you because, of the two of you, you were the only person strong enough, brave enough to stop the last-minute wedding."

Tinsley stared at him, not sure what to say. He'd been trying to look after her? What the hell? She recalled his exact words and winced. "You told me that marriage was a mistake and that we'd be divorced within a few years. That I wanted to be a bride and not a wife. That I was too young and too immature to marry. You never said anything about JT!"

Cody's eyes remained steady. "I might think he has no common sense, but he's my brother, Tinsley." He lifted an arrogant eyebrow. "Besides, was I wrong?" he asked.

Tinsley opened her mouth to blast him, but quickly realized that her impulse to defend JT was a conditioned response. "No, I guess not," she reluctantly admitted.

"You were all those things, but I was wrong to focus on your faults when I was most concerned about JT's selfishness and inability to communicate. We come from a long line of men who don't talk," Cody admitted.

Tinsley watched, fascinated, as Cody's green eyes heated with desire. "The fact that I managed to say anything with you in that dress was a minor miracle in itself. You took my breath away."

Tinsley blushed, remembering her wedding dress. Her skirt had been layers of cream-colored chiffon but her top had minimal fabric, just a series of perfectly placed appliqués covering just enough of her upper torso to avoid sending her grandfather to the hospital.

"JT was so uninterested in anything to do with the wedding, and I wanted to shock him into paying attention," Tinsley admitted.

"Did it work?" Cody asked her, looking interested.

"Not really," she again reluctantly admitted.

"Well, if it helps, I spent the duration of that sober ceremony thinking very unchurch-like thoughts about how I would strip you out of that dress," Cody told her, his voice rough with desire.

What? Really? "You were attracted to me back then?" she asked, her mouth slack with shock.

"Jesus, Tinsley…" Cody roughly responded. "I've always been attracted to you."

No…*really*? What? Tinsley stared at him, completely flummoxed. She'd never suspected, not once, that Cody thought of her as anything other than a pesky sister-in-law and pain in his butt.

"I don't know what to say to that."

Cody shrugged. "Nothing to say. It was what it was." He dropped his leg and leaned forward. "New Year's Eve was, for me, a long time coming." His lips quirked at the double entendre, but he didn't voice the obvious. "It was better than I ever imagined."

Tinsley sighed. It had been the best sexual experience of her life—one perfect, sensuous night she would remember until the day she died. But one that would never be repeated. Cody could pull strong feelings to the surface and, whether they were anger or frustration or heat or desire, she wasn't interested in dealing with wild emotions. She'd experienced too much turmoil with JT; she simply wanted calm. She'd had her one night of passion, and the memories of that would sustain her for a long, long time.

She'd spent twelve years floundering in a relationship, and she knew that getting emotionally or sexually involved with another Gallant was a terrible idea. If JT was a tropical storm, then Cody would be a category-five hurricane, and she wasn't prepared to allow another Gallant—or another man—to cause her to spin out again.

Tinsley forced herself to eat another slice of pizza before wiping her hands and mouth again with a fresh napkin. She sipped at her ginger beer and held the glass against her chest. "Do you think you and JT are both antikids because you had such little input from your dad?"

"To be fair, we didn't have that much from our mom either," Cody admitted. "She was a busy lady and didn't spend a lot of time with us."

Now that was a revelation since JT, the very few times she spoke about his mom, sang her praises, which she shared with Cody.

"JT and I are very different people, Tinsley, and I can only speak for myself. That's not how I remember her," Cody told her, folding his arms. His big biceps bulged, and the cotton of his Henley caressed the curves. *Yum.* "From the time I was twelve, I all but raised JT. I took on that responsibility."

"Because your father was mired in grief and couldn't function," Tinsley sympathetically stated.

"Wow, that's not true either. Your ex told you a Candyland version of our teenage years. Dad shrugged off Mom's death, took two weeks off to 'grieve,' then left every night around ten to spend the night with his long-term mistress. After a month, he returned full-time to work and resumed his insane travel schedule."

Bertram Gallant had been an international yacht

salesman and the Ryder-White and Gallant families initially connected through Cody's father, Tinsley remembered. "Wasn't your dad good friends with my great-uncle Benjamin, Callum's much younger brother?"

He nodded. "Ben Ryder-White and my dad were both into yachts and my father credits Ben for launching his career selling them."

"How so?" Tinsley asked, fascinated.

"Ben asked Bertram to find him a yacht suitable for a race he wanted to enter, and Bertram did. He earned a fat commission on the deal and that led to many more."

"Really? I did not know that." There were quite a few gaps in her knowledge about her family. But that didn't surprise her, since Callum never discussed Ben, who died before she was born. Tinsley did recall her father telling her and Kinga the odd tale about their great-uncle, and she got the impression that he was a wonderful man and very different from her grandfather.

She did know that Callum and Ben once ran Ryder International together, as partners. Then Callum started pressuring Ben to marry, to produce a son. Even back then, producing the next generation of Ryder-White men had been important to Callum and he'd nagged Ben to do his part. Ben finally admitted he was gay and had met the man he wanted to marry.

And her grandfather—scared of change and scandal—instigated a campaign to force Benjamin out of the day-to-day running of the family business. It worked. Ben left Ryder International and moved in with his partner, Carlo, for a short time before passing away in a tragic car accident.

Her father's support for Ben never wavered, yet another reason Callum and James didn't get along.

"I soon realized that my father wasn't lonely on those constant business trips. His mistress joined him," Cody told her, yanking her back into the present.

"My dad was a selfish guy and so am I," Cody quietly admitted. "None of us like to take responsibility."

Oh, that was a load of hooey. Cody was one of the most responsible people she knew. When he said he was going to do something, he did it. One didn't build and grow a massive company, employ thousands of people, without being accountable.

If she pointed that out, he'd just say that was business.

"You were and you still are," Tinsley told him. "As a teenager, you were more responsible than your forebears were as adults."

He stared at her before shrugging. "Maybe. But having so much pressure on me at such a young age is also why I've avoided relationships and getting tied down."

She understood why he felt like that and couldn't blame him. "That's why I'm giving you an out, Cody," Tinsley reminded him.

"I'm not sure if that's what I want anymore." Cody raked a hand through his hair and down the back of his head. Seeing something on her face—surprise? excitement?—his eyes narrowed, and his jaw hardened. "Don't get excited. I'm not about to offer to be a full-time dad or to raise the kid with you," he muttered. No, he wasn't, at least, he wasn't *yet*. But she knew he would. Sometime between now and the birth of their baby, he'd climb on board instead of holding onto a rope and being pulled along in the ship's wake. And, if she knew him, and she thought she did, he'd soon want to captain the ship.

She'd have to work out how to deal with *that*.

"Noted," she stated.

Cody's frown deepened. "I'm serious, Tinsley. Don't expect too much from me."

She didn't need to because he expected a lot from himself and there was no way he'd shirk his responsibility, to her or her child. She knew he wouldn't offer her marriage—and she didn't want him to because a baby was a terrible reason to get married!—but neither would he walk away. "I won't, Cody."

Tinsley suspected he was trying to manage her expectations of him but she also knew, somewhere down deep where truth resided, that Cody was a much better man than he gave himself credit for. His father and brother might be a little dysfunctional, but Cody Gallant had his life together.

He stood up, looked down at her plate and then to her pizza box. "God, you've hardly eaten anything.

No wonder you're on the verge of passing out every two seconds."

He'd polished off his pizza, she noticed. "I ate far more than I expected to."

Cody shook his head, closed the boxes and picked up their plates and took them through to the kitchen. Tinsley heard him putting the plates into the dishwasher, the opening and closing of the fridge. When he returned, he sat down in the chair he'd been occupying earlier.

"So, business. How did the meeting with the Food Network producer go?" he asked, placing his ankle on his opposite knee.

Tinsley pulled up her legs and wrapped her arms around her knees. "He wants some time to think about it, but he sounded keen. It's reality TV so if the contestants are dynamic and interesting, he's all-in. If the contestants are dull and boring, he's out, so he's only interested in picking up the story at the national and international level. He's not interested in the regional and state competitions."

"Neither, to be honest, are we. There's not much PR mileage in those competitions," Cody said.

"Oh, and he perked up when I told him that Jules is to be a judge. He's heard of her and would like to see her on camera." Tinsley smiled at him. "I think he has a little crush on her."

"Who doesn't?" Cody quipped.

Tinsley laughed. Unlike her reaction at the ball, she was unoffended this time around. Jules was charismatic and stunningly beautiful, and men dropped to their knees as she walked past. Tinsley was more suspicious of men who didn't have a crush on Jules than men who did. Jules was a force of nature, but she was also sweet and sincere and a crazy good friend. And Tinsley felt enormously guilty for not telling her best friend, and her sister, that she was pregnant.

She wasn't the chattiest person around, but she did talk to her sister and Jules. They knew her inside out. So why hadn't she? She'd tried, once or twice, but every time she saw them or had a moment alone with them, she couldn't get the words to form. It was the weirdest thing: she wanted to tell them but her tongue wouldn't spit out the required sentences.

Maybe it was because she still didn't feel pregnant, that the idea was lodged in her brain but for some reason, not in her heart. Was that because she was embarrassed to tell them she got pregnant via a one-night stand? Or was it because she was worried they'd think her hypocritical? After all, her ONS was Cody, the man whom she professed to detest.

Pulling her thoughts back to business, Tinsley asked whether his meeting with Geraint du Pont was successful. "Yep, he's keen to judge. As I said, he's got time on his hands, and he's waiting for his new restaurant to be built, which is going to take at least six months.

"We spoke in his kitchen, while he whipped up a quick mushroom-and-shrimp risotto," he added. One of her all-time favorite foods. Tinsley picked up a cushion from the chair behind her and threw it at his head. "You ate his risotto? I am green with envy!"

Cody caught the silk-covered cushion and tossed it onto the sofa behind her. When his eyes sparkled with amusement, he looked years younger and irresistible. The guy rocked a suit but seeing him dressed casually, in sweatpants, a well-fitting Henley and bare feet, rocked her world. The fire in the grate crackled but it was no match for the heat running through her system.

For weeks now she'd been ignoring, or denying, her need for him, pushing her attraction away. But tonight, all her barriers were crumbling and she wanted to be with him again, kissing his mouth, exploring his body, lost in him.

Lost with him.

She was tired of thinking, worrying, strategizing, planning. Tonight she wanted to *feel*…

Tinsley unfurled her body and stood up slowly, linking her hands behind her back and arching to stretch. Cody's eyes went to her chest and his gaze heated. His hands moved to the arms of his chair and his fingers pushed into the fabric as if he were trying to restrain himself from putting his hands on her.

This was fun, Tinsley thought. She hadn't thought she could have this sort of effect on him. That she possessed the power to make the muscle in his jaw tick, his eyes soften, his pants jump. It was heady… and wonderful.

"What are you doing, Tinsley?" Cody asked her, his voice deeper than it had been a few minutes before. His voice, already a rich baritone, dropped an octave or two when he was aroused. She glanced at his pants and, yep, he was interested.

Very interested indeed.

And all because she stood up and stretched. Amazing.

There was no point in being coy; Cody wouldn't appreciate it. "I'm trying to seduce you," she admitted, blushing.

Cody sat up and ran his hands over his face, as if he were trying to wipe her words away.

Tinsley wrinkled her nose. "I know. It's not a good idea, I'm pregnant, we're trying to figure things out, we work together…blah, blah, blah." Tinsley walked over to where he sat and placed her hands on the arms of his chair, forcing him to lean back. "I know, Cody, I'm living it! But just for tonight, while the snow falls outside and the world stops, I just want to…"

Arrgh, telling a man—Cody—she wanted to make love with him wasn't as easy as she'd thought it would be. What if he rejected her? She would look like a fool, and she hated feeling that way.

She stopped, uncertain of the way forward.

She'd experienced enough rejection in her life, thanks very much.

Before she could decide what to do, Cody's hand shot up to capture the back of her head and he pulled her down so that his mouth met hers. And the world, everything she knew, slid away. All she wanted was to be in his arms, surrounded by him. She leaned in close and caught a hint of his citrus-and-spice cologne. Teasing herself, and him, she ever so softly brushed her lips against his and pulled back to look at him, to judge his reaction. His lips lifted and his smile hit his eyes, warm, delicious and dazzling.

As she still leaned over him, his hand still cupped around the back of her head, they shared a long, delicious, sexy-as-hell kiss, one that went on and on and on. She moved closer, straddled his knees and sank into his broad body, trying to get as close as possible in the confines of the chair. His fingers played with her hair and rippled down her spine as their tongues danced and dueled. His body was so different to hers, hard and solid and panty-meltingly delicious. Cody's grip on her tightened and Tinsley felt lost in him, loving the unexpected intimacy of their embrace.

It was as if they'd put everything on hold, living in the now instead of in the future. It was exactly what she needed.

She loved kissing him, but she needed more, needed him to be the puzzle piece her body was missing.

As if he heard her silent pleas, Cody's hand snaked up and under her shirt and onto her lace-covered breast, impatiently pulling down the bra cup to find her hard nipple. His thumb brushed across it, applying the right amount of pressure for maximum pleasure, and she moaned, arching her back, silently begging for more. Annoyed with the barrier of fabric between them, Tinsley leaned back and swiftly removed her shirt, closing her eyes when both his hands covered her breasts. "Take it off, Cody, and put your lips on me."

Was that *her* voice? She hadn't realized she could sound demanding and sexy at the same time. Her scattered thoughts evaporated as Cody unsnapped the front clasp of her expensive bra and looked down at her chest, his eyes that stunning green that defied description. He kissed each of her breasts, twisting his tongue around her nipples. Tinsley moved so that her knees were on either side of his hips but there wasn't enough room for her to rest her aching core against his shaft, to assuage that need to be as close as possible to him. Scooting back, she stood up, unsteady and held her hand out to him.

"Take me to bed, Cody."

Cody shook his head. "No."

Disappointment shot through her, hard and fast. He didn't want her…

He gripped her jaw and tipped her head up to look at her, looking into her soul. "I can't wait that long. I need you here, now. Fast."

Oh…oh, thank God.

Cody yanked her to him and her breasts pushed against his chest, his desire for her hard against her stomach. He ducked his head and she stood on her toes, their lips locked together in another, hard, take-me-now, take-everything kiss.

Impatient, Cody stripped her clothes, then his. She

stood in front of him, surprisingly unselfconscious—
how could she feel shy when he looked at her like
she hung the moon and danced among the stars? His
hands raced over her body, over her breasts, down
her waist, slipping between her legs. She was drip-
ping with need and he released a long growl when
he sank his fingers into her warm channel. Tinsley
released a wail and found herself being turned away
from his body, Cody's large hand on her back. "Grab
the arms of the chair with your hands—lift your ass,"
he commanded.

Ridiculously excited at this new position, wondering what it would bring, she did as he asked and
then his erection slid into her and he rested his chest
against her back, holding her close with one arm
around her waist, his other hand delving between her
legs. Tinsley held on as passion soared and swirled,
feeling completely encapsulated by him.

He pushed in deeper and she felt his lips on the
side of her neck, on her shoulder. They established
a fast, wicked rhythm, and her hips rose to meet
each deep thrust. Her hands found his arms, nails
raking his skin.

Tinsley felt herself on the edge of that delicious
cusp, wanting to wait for him but knowing she
couldn't hold out much longer. Heat flashed over
her, and her low moans became tiny screams. She
felt herself losing control. He thrust deeper and his
response caused her to detonate into a fireball of
colors. She knew that he'd come but they still kept

going, unable to end this passionate tango. She felt him harden, heard his low growl and his hand slid between them again, touching that magic knot of nerves, and she flew up, exploding as she hit that fireball again.

It took a while for them to move, to speak, to unknot themselves from their sexual tangle. Cody lifted his hand to stroke her hair and dropped a brief, dazzling kiss on her mouth. "That was amazing... You are amazing..."

Tinsley blushed. "I...that...*wow*."

Cody sent her a tender smile and pulled her closer. They held each other tight, just enjoying being together. Tinsley felt his lips in her hair, on her temple and her cheek. Then he stepped back and held out his hand to her. "I have an amazing shower I'd like to show you," he told her, the light in his eyes very wicked indeed.

"I'd very much like to see your shower," Tinsley told him, walking with him up the steel-and-wood stairs. "But I'm far more interested in the fun we can get up to in it."

Nine

Their meeting was finished, and Callum had dismissed them, but instead of leaving, Tinsley stayed in her chair on the opposite side of Callum's desk. Cody turned to look at Callum, who, as always, looked characteristically uninterested. Callum Ryder was a hard man and didn't have an affectionate bone in his body. He treated his son and two granddaughters like the employees they were.

Callum's bushy white eyebrows lifted. "Is there something else, Tinsley?" he asked, his tone dismissive, as it always was.

"I've been asked by the family to encourage you to see a doctor," Tinsley quietly stated. Cody had seen Tinsley, James and Penelope in a huddle earlier in the break room, engaged in an intense discussion and it was now obvious that she'd drawn the short straw to talk to Callum. It explained Tinsley's sudden bad mood.

Callum started to respond but Tinsley spoke before he could. "We are all worried about you. Your complexion is gray, your breathing seems labored and, occasionally, your lips seem a little blue."

Callum hadn't been well for a while. Hadn't he said as much to Kinga ages ago?

Callum stared at Tinsley, displeasure in his eyes and on his face. "I am nearly eighty years old, and I do not need to be spoken to like a child."

Now that was unfair, Cody thought, walking to the closest wall and leaning his shoulder into it. Tinsley had been rather respectful in her request. Cody glanced at the door and considered leaving them alone, but he'd been on the fringes of this family for years, was a frequent guest in Callum's home and Ryder International was one of his best clients.

He would keep his mouth shut and his opinions to himself, unless the conversation turned ugly. He respected Tinsley and would let her handle her elderly relative but, client or not, he would not tolerate Callum verbally abusing his lover, the mother of his child.

"You are not well and we all would like you to seek medical advice," Tinsley said, her voice calm. Cody just managed to contain his snort, thinking that Tinsley was the pot calling the kettle black. Despite spending a lot of time together lately—in bed and out—no matter how much he begged, pleaded or demanded she take it easier, see a doctor right away, she refused. Tinsley was the most stubborn person he'd ever met. Possibly even more so than her ornery grandfather. And that was saying something.

"Callum, this is ridiculous." Tinsley stood up and placed her hands on her grandfather's desk. Callum looked at her hands, then the desk, silently demanding her to back away. Cody thought she was playing with fire; Callum wasn't someone who took orders well.

Like grandfather, like granddaughter.

"Just go and see a doctor," Tinsley told him, frustration coating her words.

"Leave me, please," Callum echoed her tone. They stared at each other for a minute before Tinsley threw her hands in the air. Stepping away from the desk, she shook her head and when she spoke, her tone was sad. "You're not an easy man to love, or to care for, Callum."

Callum looked at her, his expression blank. He finally nodded. "I know. Leave me now."

Tinsley spun around on her heel, stomped across Callum's big office and whipped open the door. After collecting her forgotten iPad, Cody followed her to her office to find her sitting behind her desk, scowling. Temper sparked in her extraordinary eyes.

"He's not well, Cody."

Cody placed the folders and the iPad on her desk and echoed her stance from earlier by placing his palms flat on her desk to look her in the eye. "You're right. He's not."

"He needs to seek medical attention."

This was his opening, and, hell yeah, he was taking it. "I agree. But you are being superbly hypocritical, sweetheart."

It took her some time for his words to make sense and when they did, fury turned her blue eyes purple. "*What* did you just say to me?"

Her face flushed and her mouth flattened and, together with the scalding anger in her eyes, he received her silent message to back way, way off. But he'd had too many arguments with this woman to be scared of one more. Cody stood up and jammed his hands into the pockets of his suit pants. "You heard me."

"I'm hypocritical? I'm *hypocritical*?"

"Repeating it a few times isn't going to change the meaning of the word, Tinsley," Cody said, keeping his temper leashed. He'd asked her for the last three weeks or so to see a doctor, to push up her appointment and get some help. But she told him it was just a phase. It would pass.

She was the most infuriating, most frustrating woman he'd ever met. But she was also the least demanding. She didn't nag him to come around, to bring her flowers, to take her out and about. He had to wrestle work away from her—she had the nasty habit of trying to do everything herself—and, if he didn't bully her to go home, she would live at the office.

She was driven and independent. And he wanted her more every day.

"You cannot possibly be equating my situation with Callum's!" Tinsley said, her voice rising. Looking past him, she nodded at the door. "Close that, please."

Oh, and she was also bossy. "Do it yourself," he mildly suggested.

Tinsley pushed her chair back, stood up and stomped over to the door, slamming it shut. Cody winced. Way to go, Ryder-White—she'd just informed everyone else on the floor they were fighting.

Cody shrugged, unconcerned. It wasn't the first time and it wouldn't be the last. Neither she, nor their arguments, scared him.

"You and Callum are both unwell and neither of you will haul your stubborn ass off to the doc." He shrugged. "So, yeah, in my mind, your situations are comparable. Except that you are being hypocritical in demanding that he seek medical attention when you won't."

Tinsley slapped her hands on her hips. "I am *pregnant*. These symptoms are a normal part of the process. As far as I know," she stated, sounding superbly sarcastic, "my grandfather isn't pregnant."

"Your symptoms are extreme, and you know it," Cody stated, clenching his fists inside his pockets.

"You are like a broken record!" Tinsley told him, her face flushed with irritation. "Can you give it a rest, please? This is my body, dammit!"

"It's my baby!" Cody shot back, pointing at her stomach. "You are carrying my child, and I need to know that you are okay, that my kid is okay."

Tinsley stared at him, obviously flabbergasted.

And so was he. Lately they'd avoided the topic of his involvement in the baby's life. He'd told her that he would pay child support and all schooling expenses, but that was as far as they got. He hadn't told her that he wanted to be a part of their child's life, *her* life.

He'd thought they had time on their side, that they could enjoy each other, enjoy living in the moment, until their burning need for each other faded away. Because that's what always happened. He wasn't a together-forever kind of guy. Sexual boredom was just taking a hell of a lot longer to settle in with her.

After their passion was spent, they'd morph into being friends—he wouldn't accept anything less— and he'd take an active role in raising their child.

He wasn't sure he could do it, but he wanted to try.

Cody saw she was looking at him, her expression a little odd, like she was waiting for an explanation. He had none to give her; his thoughts were a jumbled mess. "I should be a part of your lives," he said, groping for words. The instant the words left his mouth, he winced. They lacked conviction and he knew Tinsley would pick up on that.

"Should?" Tinsley spit the word out, rolling her eyes. "Dammit, Cody, how many times do I have to tell you that I don't need you, that we'll be fine on our own, that I am very prepared to do this single-handed?"

"You don't have to!" Cody shouted back. "I'm standing here, offering to help."

Tinsley released a hard, brittle laugh. "Really? Well, that's the first time I've heard you say that."

She shook her head and lifted her hand, palm facing front. "Seriously, don't hurt yourself making the offer. I don't need you. I don't need anybody."

"Yeah, you're so okay on your own, so stubborn in your belief that you have this all under control that you haven't told your sister or best friend or even your parents about the baby. If you are feeling so strong and so capable, why are you keeping this a secret?"

Her mouth opened and closed. He could see she was annoyed that she couldn't find a quick, cutting answer. "My relationship with my sister, my parents and my best friend is none of your business, Gallant!"

"Of course it is!" Cody closed his eyes, frustrated. "I've been in and out of your life since you were fifteen years old, Tinsley! I have eaten at your parents' and grandfather's tables, I have worked with Jules, I know all of you. So don't you dare treat me like I am some man you picked up on a whim and intend to discard when you tire of him!"

She wrinkled her nose and dropped her eyes, a sure sign that she was embarrassed. She wanted to do that, he realized. At her core, she didn't want him to step up to the plate with the baby. Because in a month or two, or three or four, she wanted to be able to walk away from him and cut him out of her life.

Tinsley wasn't interested in help or sharing responsibility. That had to be the reason she hadn't pushed him to commit to their child, because she didn't want to share control, had no interest in being half of a whole. She wanted to do what she wanted, when she wanted, to call each and every shot.

She knew he wasn't the type to stand on the sidelines, to have someone else pull his strings. He wasn't a damn puppet. He was a guy who was superbly comfortable in a leadership role, who could and did make decisions with ease.

But Tinsley wanted to do everything herself. She showed him that every day. She wanted all the control, all the time, and she knew he would never live under her direction. That was why she hadn't made any demands on him.

"You need to see someone about your issues with control, Ryder," Cody told her, pushing an agitated hand through his hair.

"What?"

Tinsley's eyes slammed into him, but he refused to look away. Yep, they were going there; she needed to know that she couldn't carry on this way.

"Seriously, you have a problem. You struggle to delegate even the smallest tasks and when you do, you micromanage them. You double-check on me, all the time. You keep telling me that you're happy to raise our baby alone but that's not because you don't want help—you just don't want to give up control."

Tinsley straightened her spine and looked at him, a cold, hard mask falling over her face. "So, I need medical *and* mental help. That's what you're saying?"

He hadn't used those terms but, yeah.

When he didn't answer, Tinsley pointed at the

door. "Get the hell out of my office, Cody. And don't you dare come back until I tell you that you can!"

Cody shook his head. "There you go again. Everything has to be on your terms, your way. That doesn't work for me, babe."

"Right now, you aren't working for me, *babe*." Tinsley walked over to the door and yanked it open, her face flushed with temper. She gestured for him to leave. When he planted his feet, her grip on the door handle tightened. "I swear to God, if you don't leave now, I *will* call security and have you escorted from the building."

Cody closed his eyes, mentally shaking his head. He'd pushed her too far. They weren't going to get anywhere today, not when she was so angry, and he was beyond frustrated too. No, it would be better to postpone this discussion to a time when they were both feeling calmer. His instinct was to stay and fight but he knew he had to be sensible. It wasn't a defeat; it was a retreat. He'd fight this battle another day, in a different way.

They would work this out—they had to. They had a baby on the way. They needed to find a way to deal with each other and to compromise. They were adults and they had time.

Cody nodded and walked to the door, stopping next to her. Her citrus-orchard scent slapped him and he felt the strong hit of desire. Her face was flushed, her lips were swollen and her eyes sparking...

And he'd never wanted her more.

Too bad, so sad.

Cody reined in his base instincts and dropped a kiss on her temple, frowning when she pulled back to avoid his touch. "We're not done with this, Tinsley. I need you to let me in, give a little, *bend*."

Tinsley, stubborn to the core, narrowed her eyes to slits and made a shooing motion. "Go."

Cody released an under-his-breath curse.

All he was doing was banging his head against a brick wall, so he went.

Later that evening, in her lovely home, Tinsley pulled a cork out of an expensive bottle of red and looked at the vol-au-vents she'd quickly assembled. Spinach and ricotta for Kinga, salmon and chives for Jules. They'd both demurred when she invited them around for an impromptu snack and wine party, saying that they had things to do, but when she told them she needed to talk, really talk, they immediately agreed to be at her place around seven.

It was ten past now.

Tinsley looked around her perfectly decorated, nothing-out-of-place house and thought, for the first time, that its perfection was cold and uninviting. But living in a messy house, with a messy person—like she had with JT, who was the biggest slob alive—made her feel anxious.

Being pregnant, her position at Ryder International, living up to her deep-seated belief that she needed to be perfect—she felt anxious, all the time.

And the more turbulent she felt inside, the more

she tried to control what was happening outside. Most people shrugged off chaos or ran away from it, but she dug in. She bossed people around and became belligerent about how things should be.

Cody was the first person to call her on that.

She'd been an anxious, sensitive child, and only felt secure when everyone around her looked or felt happy, when life was rolling along smoothly. She knew that they had to keep Callum happy, that bad things would happen if they didn't. A memory hovered, just out of reach.

If they are anything less than perfect, you will bear the consequences...

That long ago sentence, spoken by Callum when she was a child, reverberated around her skull. Was that the reason she was so anxious, the root of her need for control?

As she placed her snacks on a pretty platter, she remembered being a scared child, not wanting to put a foot wrong and disappoint her grandfather or her parents. Her hair was always tidy, her room obsessively neat, her homework always done. Order made her feel less anxious, so she strived to put everything in its box.

Her need for perfection wasn't new, or born out of JT's passive-aggression; it was something she'd lived with her whole life. She'd always liked to have everything—objects and emotions—in a box. But Cody, damn him, was unboxable. No matter how much she pushed him, he stood his ground. And her growing

feelings for him were becoming bigger and bolder.
They were bubbling over. Cody made her feel feminine and fabulous, protected and precious.

He made her feel like who she could be if she just
undid the supertight knot holding the many strands
of her life and her emotions together. But losing control petrified her, so she held fast and made herself
miserable.

God, what was she going to do? How was she
going to resolve this? Move forward?

Tinsley heard her front door open and the sound
of melodious female voices in her hallway. Walking out of her kitchen, she greeted Kinga and Jules,
kissing their cold cheeks and hugging them close.

"Thanks for coming over," Tinsley told them, as
they sat down on her couches, adorned with bright
pink and red roses. They immediately crossed their
legs, sat up straight and looked like they were at a job
interview. Tinsley remembered walking into Cody's
home, unzipping her boots and putting her feet up
on the cushions. Her sister and friend should be as
relaxed in her house as she was in his.

It was a little thing but important.

"Take off your shoes, curl up, get comfortable."

She saw the surprised look they exchanged but
ignored it, walking back into the kitchen to get the
tray of wine, glasses and vol-au-vents. She placed it
on the coffee table and Jules, brilliant mixologist that
she was, pointed out that there was a glass missing.

Tinsley perched on the edge of a chair and placed

her hands between her knees. She wrinkled her nose. "Yeah, that's why I asked you over. I need to tell you why I'm not drinking."

"Antibiotics?" Kinga asked, reaching for a vol-au-vent.

"No, I'm pregnant."

Shock flashed across their faces, as bright as the sun. Kinga placed her wineglass on the table, her mouth slack with surprise. "What? How?"

Tinsley waved her questions away. "It's a long, complicated story."

Jules sipped from her glass, calmer than her sister, and picked up a vol-au-vent. "We're listening."

"During a huge fight today, Cody told me that I should've told you guys a while back. On that he was right," Tinsley reluctantly admitted. "Actually, he was right about a whole lot of stuff," Tinsley morosely added.

Kinga waved her words away. "You're always fighting with Cody. That's nothing new. We'll come back to him, and the love-hate-love thing you've got going. Who's the fath…? Oh, crap. Is Cody the father of your baby?"

Tinsley nodded.

"I didn't think he wanted kids," Jules said, once she'd absorbed Tinsley's new reality.

"How do you know that?" Tinsley demanded, curious as to why Jules would know something so personal about Cody.

"We worked an event in Rome a few years back

and there were some kids causing havoc and he told me, in no uncertain terms, that he wasn't interested in being a dad," Jules explained. "That being said, I presume that your pregnancy was a great big oops? What happened?"

"We used condoms." Tinsley hunched her shoulders. "We genuinely don't know how it happened. Just that it did."

"Wow," Kinga said. She leaned forward and placed her hand on Tinsley's knee. "I've been so busy with the ball and with Griff that I've neglected you, Tins. I thought you looked tired and wan, but I never suspected this. I'm so sorry I haven't been there for you."

"Me too," Jules added, guilt in her eyes.

"It's not your fault, guys. I could've told you at any time during these past few weeks."

"Why didn't you?" Jules asked her, looking at the snack in her hand. "God, these are delicious. Have one."

Salmon? Cheese? The smell? Uh…no, thank you.

"Because I am being completely, irrationally anxious about my pregnancy and if I told you I was pregnant then I'd have to admit something else, something I don't want to face."

At her serious tone, their attention sharpened and their bodies tensed. "What, Tins?"

Tinsley walked into the kitchen and picked up two pregnancy tests lying on the counter. She showed them to Jules and Kinga. "I did these this morning and they both say that I'm pregnant, right?"

"Uh…yeah," Jules answered for them both.

"From around six weeks I have been vomiting constantly, I am extremely tired, my breasts feel like someone has stabbed them with a curling iron."

Kinga pulled a face.

"I've never felt as crap as I have the last few weeks, but those are all symptoms of being pregnant, right?"

"If you say so," Kinga replied, her tone soothing. "I'm not sure what you are trying to tell us, sweetie."

If Tinsley said this out loud, there was no going back. There was no brushing this off as her anxiety working overtime, or just the normal worry about her baby's development. If she articulated this, she'd have to deal with how she felt. And she didn't want to.

The urge to run away and bury her head in the sand was strong.

"The tests say I'm pregnant, my body is acting like I'm pregnant but I don't think I'm pregnant."

Kinga and Jules looked equally confused. "We don't understand, Tinsley."

She didn't either, not really. All she knew was that there was something very amiss with the pregnancy… She knew this like she knew her name.

And at her appointment tomorrow, the ultrasound would confirm it. She'd leave her doctor's office without a baby—that she knew for sure. And she'd have to go back to her life that wasn't really a life, filled with pressure and stress and anxiety.

She and Cody had been tied together by the pregnancy and the cocktail competition but, in a month or two, Cody's staff would take over the day-to-day operation of the competition and her time with Cody would be curtailed. The cords binding them would snap and she would be on her own.

Without a baby.

She couldn't bear the thought. She couldn't imagine a life without Cody in it. Because he was so honest, so direct and such a protector, she felt safe with him, happy to allow him to take the wheel, hold the reins. He was the least passive-aggressive person she'd ever met and she trusted him to do what he said he would, to be an adult and to consider her opinions and observations. With him, she never felt like an afterthought.

He was stable, thoughtful and responsible and being around him made her feel calm, kept her anxiety under control. With Cody she forgot to run what-if scenarios, to plan for every potential possibility; she trusted him to handle things as they came along. With him, the urge to micromanage—he wouldn't let her anyway!—faded.

He was the yin to her yang, the calm to her storm.

She loved him, as she'd never loved anyone before.

But Cody didn't want a child or a partner and, while she knew he didn't want something to be wrong with the baby, a part of him would be relieved not to have the responsibility of a child. And he would be glad to stop working with her. She was difficult and controlling and annoying.

Hell, she frequently wanted to run far away from herself too.

"Something is wrong with the baby, with the pregnancy," Tinsley repeated the words and felt the truth on her tongue.

"Are you sure you're not just overreacting, Tins?" *Because we know that you often do.*

Tinsley heard the unspoken subtext in her sister's voice. It was a valid point. Maybe she was. Maybe she was just scared and feeling overwhelmed and anxious.

Maybe.

"I really hope I am being irrational, Kingaroo," Tinsley told her, tears gathering in her throat. "I have an appointment tomorrow. I guess I'll find out then."

Kinga cursed. "Crap, Tins, I am leaving for Monaco early tomorrow to meet with the organizers of the yacht race Ryder International is sponsoring. You asked me to do that, remember?"

Yeah, she did.

"And I'm leaving for Cancun on a red-eye tonight," Jules told her. "But Cody will be with you, so you won't be on your own."

"Cody doesn't know the appointment is tomorrow and I'm not going to tell him. If something is wrong, I need time to process it on my own before I tell him."

They both looked horrified. "That's not a good idea, Tinsley. This isn't something you should do alone," Jules insisted.

But it was. At some point, she was going to have to live the rest of her life alone, without Cody, so she might as well get used to doing the hard stuff on her own right away. There was no point easing into it.

She needed to relearn how to be on her own again, to not to be part of a couple, to get on without a man in her life. She needed to face her anxiety and deal with it. Become healthier and happier.

All on her own. It was her inner work. Cody couldn't do it for her.

"I'll be fine, I promise. If the baby is fine, I'll be ecstatic. If it isn't, I'll be okay because I've mentally prepared for that possibility."

"I'm sure it's just your anxiety getting the best of you," Kinga told her, trying to reassure her. "Everything will be fine, I promise."

Tinsley made herself smile, knowing that, on this occasion, Kinga was wrong. Yeah, she was anxious, but her feelings about her baby went deeper than that. It was her soul speaking.

Her soul was also telling her to face this alone. Because if she was denied her wish for a child and stopped herself from falling apart, she knew she could deal with pretty much anything.

Even Cody leaving her life.

Ten

Since Kinga sent him a text message telling him that Tinsley had a doctor's appointment this morning, Cody realized that nothing he'd said to Tinsley had registered.

Zip. Zero. Nada.

Cody looked at his watch as he approached the waiting room. He was eight minutes late for the appointment. That would do, he thought. He hadn't wanted to ambush Tinsley in the waiting room, wanting to avoid a public argument.

I'm perfectly capable of doing this on my own.
You don't need to be here.

He frowned. At some point, she needed to understand that he *wanted* to be in her life, sharing the good and bad moments, the circumstances that made them smile, others that made them weep. They were better together and the sooner she wrapped her head around that concept, the sooner they could move the hell on.

He wanted her in his bed, his hands on her body, watching their baby grow. And if she had any ideas about them living apart, well, he'd quickly disabuse her of those notions. They could live in his place—it was bigger—or in hers, but if neither option suited, they'd buy a damn house where they'd have room for a growing family.

This was only baby number one, and he intended to have a whole bunch more with that stubborn, infuriating, annoying woman.

The woman he couldn't live without.

Cody banged his hand against the door, walked into the reception room and up to the counter. He explained who he was, was directed where to go and a few minutes later he knocked on a door. A gowned technician opened the door and he introduced himself before looking past her to Tinsley, sitting up on the hospital bed, her eyes wide with surprise.

An *I'm so busted* look crossed her face.

"What are you doing here?" she squeaked, flustered.

He nodded to the nurse before speaking.

"I wanted to be here for the first scan. That isn't unusual, is it?" He kept his voice bland. During the long conversation they'd soon have, he'd explain that this was *their* kid, that he was in for the long haul and that she couldn't shut him out, not anymore.

Not with anything.

The technician told him where to stand, on the other side of Tinsley, where he had a good view of the screen. The technician pulled down Tinsley's pants and lifted her shirt, showing them her still mostly flat stomach.

"I'm going to put jelly on your tummy—it will be cold," the tech told Tinsley, smiling. She squirted a gel onto Tinsley's stomach, picked up an instrument and fiddled with the machine's keyboard. In seconds, a black-and-white image appeared on the screen.

He had no freaking idea what he was looking at.

The technician moved the probe over Tinsley's stomach and he watched her tense, saw the way her lips pinched. He wasn't the most perceptive guy in the world, but he felt the steady increase of tension in the room, a cool blanket of dread.

Tinsley lifted her hand to touch his chest but kept her eyes on the technician's face. "I think you need to call the doctor now," Tinsley told her, in a calm voice.

"What's going on?" Cody demanded as the door shut behind the technician.

Tinsley tipped her head to the side and sent him a small smile. "I'm glad you're here, Cody. I thought I wanted to be alone, but I don't. Not right now."

They could get into all that later because, right now, he wanted to know what the hell was going on. "Why is she calling the doctor?"

Tinsley's hand moved from his chest to his hand.

She linked her fingers with his and tipped her head up to look at the ceiling.

"You're pretty much the only person I could imagine being here, right now. Even though your eyes are sparking with irritation, and impatience is radiating out of every pore, you calm me. It's the weirdest thing."

Cody looked down at her. "Can we discuss this later? Where the hell is the doctor?"

The door opened and Cody turned to see a petite Asian woman walking into the room, followed by the ultrasound technician. The doctor greeted Tinsley, introduced herself to him and then stood in front of the machine, exuding calm capability.

She put more gel on Tinsley's stomach, told the tech to hit the lights and pushed the probe into Tinsley's skin, her actions speaking of competency and practice. After a few minutes of moving the probe and tapping away at the keyboard, she ordered the lights to be switched back on. Then she looked at Tinsley, sympathy in her dark brown eyes.

"I think what you have is an anembryonic pregnancy, more commonly known as a blighted ovum, Tinsley."

Tinsley nodded. Cody released a sharp puff of air and slapped his hands on his hips. "What does that mean?"

Sympathetic eyes met his. "We expect to see certain things in a scan, but I see nothing. There's just an empty sac. There's no yolk sac, no fetal pole and no heartbeat. There's fluid in the sac, so I don't think the pregnancy ever implanted."

"I don't understand," Cody said, his hands flat on the bed. "Are you saying that there's a problem with the baby?"

"I'm saying that there never was a baby, Mr. Gallant."

Bullshit! What the hell was she talking about?

"I watched and listened to her hurl her guts out! The pregnancy tests all said she was pregnant. She's also been dead tired for the past few months."

The doctor nodded. "So, basically what happens is that the body thinks there is a pregnancy and it does everything it can to support the pregnancy it assumes has implanted. The HCG and progesterone levels rise, trying to get the baby to grow. When it doesn't, the hormones up their production, leading to ever-worsening pregnancy symptoms. At some point, probably sometime very soon, Tinsley's brain will get the message that there isn't a baby and she will, in essence, miscarry."

"I'll miscarry a baby that wasn't there," Tinsley said, sounding very far away.

"You sound very calm, Tinsley. Are you okay?"

Tinsley looked at the doctor and nodded. "I thought it was my anxiety playing tricks on me, but I've known for a while that something was wrong. I didn't want to come in sooner because I didn't want you to confirm it."

So that was why she hadn't pushed him about his role in their lives, why they hadn't had any conversations about how they were going to raise this child together. She'd believed there was a problem but, true to form, didn't let him in on her suspicions. She'd kept it to herself, just like everything else.

Jesus, he couldn't live like this. He couldn't spend his life fighting to get closer, begging her to let him in.

"You can either wait for the miscarriage or I can give you something to stimulate it. Or we can do a small surgical procedure. I'll give you guys a moment to decide. When you are ready, join me."

He barely heard the doctor's words, dimly realizing that she'd left the room and the door closed behind her. He turned back to face Tinsley and watched her clean the gunk off her stomach with a paper towel, her movements calm and methodical.

When Tinsley looked at him, her eyes were clear but he noticed the churning maelstrom of pain threatening to overwhelm her. He stepped forward to hold her because, God, he needed the emotional connection, but she held her hand up to keep him at a distance.

She pulled in a deep breath, her shoulders lifted and stayed around her ears. "Well, guess that's that."

What the hell did that mean?

Tinsley pulled down her shirt and swung her feet off the bed, her face marble white in the bright light of the clinical room.

Cody gripped the edge of the bed. Jesus Christ. His baby was gone. He felt shocked and blindsided, since he'd never, not once, thought that anything would go wrong. Tinsley, obviously, had, but she'd never once hinted at that possibility.

"Why didn't you talk to me about your suspicions about there being something wrong with the baby?" he demanded, his voice tight and cold. He couldn't remember when last he'd felt this angry.

"What could you have done?"

"Forced you to see a doctor earlier. Maybe, if you didn't have this go-alone attitude, there might have been something the doctors could've done."

Tinsley's eyes widened in her pale face. "That's not fair, Cody."

"No, what's not fair is you treating this entire situation like I'm of no importance, that my opinion doesn't matter, that I'm not worthy of you sharing your innermost thoughts and worries! I asked you, time and again, to see someone."

God, she went through weeks of hell for nothing. If they'd known sooner, she could've been spared all the vomiting and the tiredness and the headaches.

The thought made him want to punch a wall.

"I'm not sure what to say to you right now, Cody," Tinsley said, looking like she was about to break into a million pieces. He knew she was trying to hold her breaking pieces together, but he was hurting too.

She pushed her shaking hand through her hair. "Look, I might've suspected that something was wrong, but I didn't *know*. I thought it was my anxiety, me overreacting. I should've told you—you're right about that.

But I have just heard that I'm not pregnant so can we postpone this fight? And the doctor is waiting for us."

Us? There was no us. There never had been. Not really. Cody shook his head, desolate at the idea of losing the baby he hadn't thought he wanted, angry at himself for losing his cool with Tinsley, devastated because he knew they could never be together. If she couldn't share this with him, a profound event that linked them together, what hope did they have of creating anything meaningful and long-lasting in the future?

It was impossible. *They* were impossible.

He might as well call it. Whatever they had was over.

He shook his head. "You go and talk to her. As you said, it's your body, your decision."

"You're not going to come with me?"

"I wasn't supposed to be here in the first place, remember? I had to get a text message from your sister." He shrugged before picking up his jacket and slinging it over his arm. "You knew that losing the baby was a possibility and you obviously thought you could handle this on your own. So handle it, Tinsley. Because being on your own is what you do best, right?"

Without looking at her, Cody walked to the door and yanked it open. His throat felt tight and his brain felt too big for his head. His heart was threatening to jump out of his chest. He needed fresh air, a drink.

To cry.

He never bloody cried, but this time, he thought he just might.

* * *

A few days later, in her parent's living room in their private wing of Callum's house, Tinsley sat on the seat in the bay window and stared at the churning waters beyond Dead Man's Cove.

She recalled spending winter days in this exact position, her attention alternating between her book and the awesome views. Though to be honest, every room in Callum's house had an awesome view, even her childhood bedroom.

Tinsley looked up as Kinga approached, carrying what Tinsley hoped was a cup of hot chocolate. Her sister had been there when she woke up from the anesthetic after her small procedure, telling her their parents were in the waiting room. When she was discharged, nobody asked her whether she wanted to go home. They just bundled her into a limousine and took her back to her childhood home, where, her mom told her, they could keep an eye on her.

Why, she had no idea. It was a quick, uncomplicated operation. She would be tender today and much better tomorrow. Right as rain the day after that.

Or as right as she could be without a baby or Cody in her life.

Tinsley squeezed her eyes closed, trying to push the pain away, opening them when Kinga nudged her knee. She looked up to see her sister carrying their favorite mugs from their childhood and smiled. Kinga had returned from Monaco and had taken time off work to be with her and she so appreciated her sister's presence. Jules, who was working in Cancun, had sent her a dozen text messages and they'd arranged to video call later. Her parents, she had no doubt, were in the kitchen, wanting to give the sisters some time alone.

"Scoot up," Kinga told her. Tinsley did as she was told and shifted to make space for Kinga on the window seat. Kinga handed Tinsley her cup—buttercup yellow—and with her free hand, pulled up the white cashmere blanket.

"How are you doing, sister?"

Tinsley stared down at her hot chocolate and sipped. Kinga, bless her, had laced it with whiskey and she started to push it away, thinking it was bad for the baby. Then she remembered and her eyes filled. Laying her head on Kinga's shoulder, she kept her eyes on the bay, thinking that she was like that water, churning and messy, unable to stop herself from smacking against the rocks at the bottom of the cliff.

"I'm okay, physically. I'm sore but it's nothing serious."

"And emotionally?" Kinga asked her.

"I'm gutted," Tinsley admitted.

"The next time I see Gallant I am going to dismember him with a rusty, blunt knife," Kinga said, her voice a low growl.

Tinsley shook her head. "It's not his fault, Kinga. I should've told him I was worried about the baby, should've told him I had an appointment with the doctor. I should've let him in, let him help, let him be there for me. I made this bed. I have to lie in it."

She didn't blame Cody for being angry; she really didn't. She'd done everything she could to push him away, consistently telling him that she was happy to ride this rollercoaster alone. She couldn't blame him for doing as she asked.

But God, she missed him. Missed his strong arms and reassuring voice, the way his eyes crinkled when he smiled and turned that deep, dark green when he was aroused. It had been nearly a week since he stormed out of the doctor's practice and she hadn't heard or seen him since. She missed him, intensely, overwhelmingly.

With Cody, she could be herself: messy, emotional, *imperfect*.

God, she'd so liked the person she was with him and she adored him. Simply loved him as she'd never loved anyone before. He was a functioning adult, someone she didn't need to look after or take care of. When they were together, she felt like she had a partner. Someone she could rely on, someone who would never let her down.

Kinga put her hand on Tinsley's knee and Tinsley saw the flash of light in her kick-ass engagement ring. "Where's Griff today?"

"He told me I needed to be with you and that he was going to spend the day working on his new album," Kinga told her. "I'm so sorry it didn't work out between you and Cody, Tins, since I believe he's the right Gallant brother for you."

Tinsley wrinkled her nose. "Jeez, can you imagine what the Portland gossips would say if they heard I'd moved on to another Gallant?"

"JT lives in Hong Kong and even if he did live in the States, he and Cody are not close so I don't see you spending Christmas and Thanksgiving with the man. And who the hell cares what the gossips say?" Kinga demanded. "Let them talk! It's your happiness I'm most concerned about."

Her sister would always be in her corner, prepared to wade into the ring to fight her battles. She so appreciated her unconditional love. Tinsley heard footsteps and saw her parents walking toward them, identical worried frowns on their faces.

Her mom stopped and put a hand on her heart. "I have a dozen memories of the two of you, sitting just like you are."

Kinga gestured to the view. "It's a pretty special place."

Tinsley watched as her dad pulled over a chair for her mom to sit, choosing to lean his shoulder into the wall. She sipped her hot chocolate, feeling the burn of whiskey, and rested the back of her head on the cool pane of glass. "I'm sorry I didn't tell you about the pregnancy."

"Why didn't you?" her mom asked, hurt in her eyes.

Tinsley scratched the back of her neck. "I thought

I would wait until I had the scan. I wasn't sure why I felt the need to keep it a secret, but I think, subconsciously, I knew something was wrong."

"As long as you didn't think we would castigate you for an unplanned pregnancy," James said.

"I never thought you would reprimand me since I am an adult, but I did think you'd be disappointed," Tinsley admitted.

"Nothing you do can ever disappoint us, darling."

Tinsley looked at her mom and lifted her eyebrows. "Mom, come on. That's a bit rich. You know that, from the time we were little, you had very high expectations for us," Tinsley snapped, wincing at her overly emotional response.

Her parents exchanged puzzled glances. "What are you talking about?"

She thought about holding back, about standing down and then remembered that was why Cody had walked, because she refused to talk, to let people in. Maybe this was a good time to start opening up. "We had to excel academically, be neat and tidy, be organized and polite."

Kinga looked at her as if she'd grown green scales. "No, we didn't." When Tinsley frowned at her, she shrugged. "Tins, they gave us a hard time if we didn't work hard, but they never demanded we be exceptional."

A frown pulled Penelope's perfectly arched eyebrows together. "You're confusing us with your grandfather. I remember your father and I telling you to *stop* working so hard, to give yourself a break, to have some fun."

"That's true. You were pain-in-the-ass driven," Kinga commented, taking Tinsley's cup from her shaking hand and handing it to her father.

Tinsley frowned. It was as if a curtain had been pulled on her memories and what she thought was true was an indistinct collage of thoughts, emotions and pictures that now didn't make any sense.

Tinsley pulled up her knees and wrapped her arms around her legs. She looked at her dad. "I have a memory of hiding under the desk in Callum's study and you two came in. You argued about Callum's will and Callum said we had to be perfect, or you would bear the consequences. What did he mean by that?"

James looked gutted. "Jesus, I didn't know you were there."

"Yeah, that's obvious," Kinga stated. "It's a conversation that Tins remembers clearly from a long time ago, so it impacted her. What were you talking about, Dad?"

James looked past their heads, his gaze on the open water beyond the point. Penelope stared at the floor, her hands gripping the arms of her chair. *Enough of this*, Tinsley thought. Moving past her sister, she dropped her feet onto the floor and stood up, feeling the twinge in her abdomen. She placed her hand on her stomach and winced. Right, no quick movements.

"Mom, Dad...this has to end! What is going on

with you two?" Tinsley demanded. When neither of them looked at her, she carried on speaking. "You two have been jumpy since Christmas and we're over it."

"Leave it alone, Tinsley," Penelope begged.

She was about to agree but then she shook her head. "No, I'm not going to leave it alone. If I felt secure enough to come out from under that desk and ask you what you were talking about, I wouldn't have spent the past twenty-plus years trying to be perfect, to not rock the boat. I've been anxious all my life and I think some of that could've been avoided if we'd communicated more. There's so much family history that's been ignored. We have too many secrets. We need to talk about them…" Tinsley insisted. "I think it's time we started being up-front, direct."

Like Cody.

A person always knew where they stood with Cody and, up until this moment, Tinsley never realized how much she'd appreciated his blunt honesty.

Tinsley felt Kinga behind her and when her sister's arm came to rest around her waist, she leaned into her strength. "Tinsley's right. What is going on and what don't we know?"

There was another long exchange of looks between James and Penelope, and a silent conversation. Wow, they might not be affectionate or lovey-dovey, but they did possess the skill of speaking to each other without using words. Was that something you learned after being married for more than thirty-five years?

James walked over to Penelope and put his hand on her shoulder. He looked at Tinsley, his expression regretful. "I am so sorry you felt pressured to be perfect. That was never our intention. And yes, we have been acting strange—it's been a strange time. Your mother and I need to talk, to be honest with each other. Maybe then we'll tell you what we can."

That wasn't good enough. They needed to know everything now. "Dad, enough with the secrets. They aren't doing anybody any good. Let's get everything out in the open—"

Tinsley frowned when three phones beeped with message alerts. Hers was in her back pocket and still switched off. Her parents and Kinga all reached for their phones and she saw identical expressions of disbelief and horror on their faces. Oh, God, something had happened. Something bad.

Kinga handed Tinsley her phone and Kinga read the message. It was from Cody.

Callum collapsed in his office about a half hour ago. He's been taken by ambulance to the Maine Medical Center. They suspect a heart attack, possibly accompanied by a mild stroke. I'm heading there now, suggest you do the same.

Callum? It wasn't possible.

But, since her dad was calling for a driver, her

sister was calling Griff and her mom was gathering their coats, it seemed the impossible had happened.

James, followed by Penelope, rushed into the foyer of the hospital and headed for the front desk. His heart was about to jump out of his chest and a headache threatened to blow his head apart. He reached back and took Penelope's hand in his. His wife might not be the great love of his life but for the past three decades and more, she'd been his rock, his anchor, his best friend.

He needed her now. His father was irascible and difficult, hard and uncompromising, but he was still his dad.

James heard his name. He whirled around to see Cody striding toward them, a worried expression on his face.

James rushed to meet him, feeling overwhelmed. So much had happened recently—Callum's machinations, Kinga getting engaged, Tinsley losing her and Cody's baby, Callum collapsing—and he felt close to breaking.

Something had to change, he decided. He couldn't live like this anymore.

Cody gripped his hand and gave Penelope a quick hug. Pulling back, he folded his arms across his chest. "They're prepping Callum for surgery. They want to do a triple bypass and they want to do it quickly."

"But?" Penelope asked, frowning.

"But Callum is being obstreperous. He refuses to consent to the operation until he's spoken to you, James."

James swore and shoved his hand through his hair. "Really? What can be so important that he's delaying a lifesaving operation?"

"It has to be something to do with Ryder International. Nothing else is that important to him," Penelope muttered. "Stubborn old bastard."

James agreed. His father was a piece of work. "Where is he?" he asked Cody.

Cody gave him directions to where Callum was waiting. "Callum said to send you, James, and no one else," Cody said, sounding sympathetic.

Penelope's smile was bitter. She took a half step back and gestured for him to leave. "You'd better get to it, James."

James nodded before dropping a quick kiss on her cheek. "Wait for me. I shouldn't be long." He looked at Cody and frowned. "And you and I, Gallant, need to talk."

Cody looked like James had pushed him against an electric fence. "I don't think…uh… I'm pretty busy at the moment."

James sent him a hard stare, the one he borrowed from Callum on rare occasions when he wanted to get his point across. "That wasn't a suggestion, Gallant."

James walked away from his wife and the man he hoped might eventually become his son-in-law.

He'd always had his reservations about JT, but Cody was a man who could handle the strong-willed and independent Tinsley. They would, if they managed to push their pride aside, have a happy life together.

As James made his way to his father, he thought about his daughters. They were, in all ways that counted, independent. They had men in their lives who loved them. Cody wasn't going anywhere; of that, James was certain. And, thanks to the trust funds he'd set up for them, they were financially independent of both their men and Ryder International. They were educated and hardworking. If everything fell apart, they would easily find work in another company. Hell, they could set up their own PR firm.

He was still tangled up with Ryder International. His fortunes still lay with the company, under his father's control. He stopped briefly, hesitating. How true was that statement, really? Was he as dependent on his father as he believed? He'd earned a spectacular salary from Ryder International but he'd also bought and sold property all his adult life, making a tidy profit along the way.

If he separated himself from Callum, he might lose the use of the private jets, the apartments in New York and Paris. They'd have to move into one of their many properties or buy another house, but they had more than enough money to do that without even feeling even the hint of a pinch.

Penelope had money from her parents, tens of millions that had not, as far as he knew, been touched. If they stayed together—and he thought they should—they'd be fine. In fact, they'd be free.

There's so much family history that's been ignored. We need to talk about it...

Tinsley was right.

He needed to get his integrity back, to find his spine, to stand up for what was right. His actions might infuriate Callum and might lead to James being excommunicated and disinherited—and his daughters not being acknowledged as the Ryder-White heirs. But, really, was that the worst thing?

He knew what their answer to that question would be: *Hell, no.* Neither of them wanted to run the empire; they'd told him that on more than one occasion, and if Callum disinherited them, he didn't think they'd much care.

His lovely daughters respected truth and openness and honesty, and he knew their respect for him would rise exponentially if he confronted the truth.

Callum wouldn't appreciate it, but he remembered how good he'd felt standing up to his father as a young adult. He'd known that defending his uncle Ben would result in blowback, but he'd done it anyway because it had been the *right* thing to do.

He'd had more courage in his twenties than he'd had in the last thirty years combined. And he was done with being scared of his father, of his power and of what punishment he could inflict.

It was time to do what was right...

James walked onto the patient floor and was immediately accosted by a stern-looking nurse, who grabbed his elbow and marched him down a corridor. "Your father is the most stubborn, ornery man I've ever met."

Welcome to my world. "He is."

The nurse nodded to a room and told him he had five minutes. James thanked her and slipped into the dark space, his eyes immediately going to the frail figure in the bed. James approached, thinking Callum looked smaller and older. He stood next to the bed and looked down and cleared his throat.

"You wanted to see me, Callum?"

Callum didn't turn his head to look at him. "You took your sweet time getting here. They are waiting to save my life, you know."

If he could've sprouted wings and flown, he wouldn't have been able to get here quicker, and Callum knew it. "We don't have much time and they need to start working on you," James said, keeping his voice even.

Callum sighed, coughed and winced, obviously in a great deal of pain. Maybe he'd called James here to apologize for his past actions, for treating him like a servant, for being such a bastard. Maybe this attack was a wake-up call and in the last few years of Callum's life, he could have a relationship with his father...

Callum turned his head and James stepped back at the intensity that blazed within his eyes. "I'm going to be out of commission for a few months. The doctors have already told me that I won't be back for at least six weeks, probably more."

James nodded. "That's okay. I'll look after the business for you."

Callum released a half laugh, half growl. "The hell you will. You don't have the balls to run Ryder International. No, I need you to find an experienced CEO, someone who takes no crap, someone who can make the hard decisions." He lifted his hand and pointed a bony finger somewhere in the direction of James's face. "That's not you, boyo."

Of course it wasn't. What had he been thinking?

"And keep working on finding out who owns my useless brother's shares, I will not tolerate any more excuses in that regard." Callum muttered, his energy and voice fading. "And get on to that DNA ancestry company and find out why we still don't have the results of those tests."

Shares and DNA tests? That was what he was worried about right now? Seriously, his father's priorities were screwed.

"Yeah, Callum, whatever," he told him.

"Promise you'll appoint a good CEO, James," Callum said, his voice a harsh whisper.

James met his father's eyes and nodded. Oh yeah, he'd appoint a kick-ass CEO. And, in the process, he'd kick over a hornet's nest.

He couldn't wait.

Eleven

The last time Penelope met with her private investigator had been in a trucker's diner in a less salubrious part of town. To hell with that now. If anyone she knew wanted to ask why she was meeting with a PI, they could damn well ask her to her face.

And she'd tell them to mind their own business.

She was over giving people explanations on subjects that didn't concern them.

In her favorite coffee shop, Penelope leaned back in the elegant chair, crossed her legs and wished she could light up a cigarette. Ben had taught her to smoke thirty-five years ago, and how to hand-roll her cigarettes. She wondered if she could still do it.

Back when she first met him, she thought him to

be a really sweet guy, oh-so-charming and consid-
erate. The exact opposite of his hard-as-nails, am-
bitious brother and so very much like her husband.

But she'd been young and people were rarely so
one dimensional.

A waiter deposited her espresso in front of her and
she nodded her thanks. Callum had come through
his triple bypass but, a week on, there were compli-
cations and he was still in the intensive care unit. He
was, according to James, conscious but weak and
didn't have the energy to talk.

Penelope sighed. Callum was a difficult man and
not easy to love. And he'd always made their lives
more complicated than they needed to be...

But had he? Years before she married James,
she'd chosen to sleep with her baby's father. She'd
thought that she couldn't possibly fall pregnant, that
bad things didn't happen to nice girls like her.

After she left the country for six months and gave
birth in London, she returned to the East Coast and
met James. Both Callum and her parents pushed them
to marry and when James proposed, she agreed, despite knowing there was a close connection between
him and the father of the baby she'd just given up for
adoption. She'd kept secrets and she'd made choices
and not everything could be blamed on Callum.

James had made his move, and Penelope still
wasn't sure whether he'd chosen the right person
to run Ryder International. But it was James's decision and she respected him for taking action. In fact,

she'd never respected her husband more. And with respect came renewed attraction, something else that surprised her.

Her decisive, clear-eyed, determined husband turned her on...

"Good morning, ma'am."

Penelope's head shot up and encountered the lovely face of the PI she'd hired. Instead of the battered jeans and hoodie she'd worn previously, KJ Holden looked like a young professional dressed in a gray-and-white houndstooth suit and with her long hair pulled back into a soft roll.

"You clean up well," Penelope commented, gesturing for her to take a seat.

KJ flashed a wide smile and sat down. "Different situations call for different clothing. I'm going to pull on my homeless-lady outfit later for a stakeout," KJ cheerfully told her.

Penelope shuddered. "Isn't that dangerous?"

"Not as dangerous as dressing up as a prostitute," KJ told her on an easy grin. "There are some weird people out there."

She could imagine.

KJ thanked the waitress for the coffee she received—she must've ordered it on her way in—and lifted the cup to take a sip. "So, I presume you want an update." KJ leaned forward and dropped her voice so she couldn't be overheard by people at the adjacent tables. "I contacted the agency you used to facilitate the adoption of your son and they stonewalled me. They refused, as

I expected, to give me any information and nothing I did or said moved them."

Penelope looked at her, surprised at the intense disappointment she felt. She'd known this would happen, as she'd made a direct appeal to the adoption agency a few weeks ago and had the exact same response. Why did she think a PI making inquiries would sway them?

Penelope rubbed her smooth forehead with the tips of her fingers, feeling let down and saddened. Had she really believed KJ could perform miracles? Was she that gullible?

It had only been three weeks since she'd first met with KJ and sent her on a mission to find her biological son. Had she conned herself into thinking that the young PI could succeed where Penelope failed?

KJ was working for a paycheck, thinking that she was trying to reunite a mother and her lost child. She had no idea that Penelope was trying to keep her reputation intact.

KJ didn't know, and Penelope would never tell her that the boy she was looking for, who was now a grown man of thirty-five, had the ability to upend her life. He held the power to expose her secrets, to make her family look at her differently for her youthful actions.

Him coming back into her life would make her husband and her daughters question her honesty and her judgement. Her daughters were independent, gutsy women with a strong moral code and she couldn't bear them looking at her with questions in their eyes, disdain on their faces.

And James! Despite thirty-plus years of marriage, James would feel gutted on hearing that she'd given birth to *someone else's* child...

That she'd kept this from him for so very long.

Her son's presence would also upend Ryder International... Of that she had no doubt.

"Have you made any progress at all? Do you have anything new you can tell me?"

KJ looked down at her notes. "I did manage to track down your case worker at the time. She's in her seventies now but she remembered you well. Apparently, you were what she called 'a complicated case.'"

That didn't surprise her in the least. "What did she have to say?"

"That you weren't the only person to contact them wanting to discover the child's real identity."

What? Really?

"Tell me more," Penelope demanded.

"There isn't that much more to tell and trust me, it took me about three hours to pry this much information from the retired case worker."

Penelope didn't bother asking her name, she didn't remember anyone from that agency and knew KJ wouldn't tell her anyway.

"Tell me everything she said," Penelope said, through gritted teeth.

KJ's calm expression didn't change. "She made it clear she would not tell me who adopted him or who he was now. She did say that she had a meeting with the boy and his parents when he was eighteen and that he was given the letter you wrote to him, informing him of his parentage. He wasn't in the least interested in opening that letter. The caseworker remembers him as a brooding, intense child.

"He has your name, Mrs. Ryder-White, and it's up to him to contact you. That's the only way you will discover his identity."

Penelope slapped her hand down on the table, making the coffee cups shake. "You implied that someone else inquired about his identity. Who?"

KJ wrinkled her nose. "Not a who, but a what. A couple of years after the adoption, an exchange of letters took place between the agency and a law firm, and they concerned the child."

"What are you talking about?" she demanded, her voice rising.

KJ gripped her right hand and squeezed. Penelope tried to pull her hand out of her grip, but the younger woman was stronger than she looked. "Ma'am, people are looking at you and I know that's not what you want. Take a breath!"

KJ's harsh words slapped her and Penelope's shoulders slumped as they penetrated. God, she was losing it, something she couldn't afford to do. This was all too complicated, too much to deal with.

"I'm sorry. Carry on."

"The case worker either had no knowledge of the contents of the letters or wouldn't tell me." KJ sighed, determination in her eyes. "I need to talk plainly, ma'am. The terms of the adoption were pretty simple, you never named the father and you gave the baby up. We can assume that the father of the child found out about the adoption, somewhere and somehow."

From her, dammit.

"But the supposed father had no legal recourse to find out the baby's identity or to overturn the adoption. Even his law firm, Gerard and Pinkler, were firmly rebutted."

Gerard and Pinkler...where had she heard that name before?

"I took the initiative to send the lawyers a letter, telling them that you'd hired me and asking whether they could provide me with any additional information."

Penelope leaned forward. "And? "

"I received a formal acknowledgement of the letter, nothing else."

Penelope slumped back in her seat. "So, we're at a dead end."

KJ nodded. "I think that's a fair statement. The ball is in your son's court, Mrs. Ryder-White. But whether he plays it or not, I cannot say."

Gerard and Pinkler...why couldn't she place that name?

She needed to do some investigating, think this through. Something hovered at the back of her mind, misty and unsubstantial. Lifting her eyes to meet

KJ's, she slowly nodded. "Let me know if the law firm contacts you again."

"Of course."

Sympathy flashed in the PI's eyes. "This must be so difficult for you, I'm so sorry."

She didn't need sympathy, she needed a resolution. To mitigate disaster or, at the very least, prepare herself for the fall out. Her world, and her family's, was going to be flipped on its head. And all because she couldn't control her emotions.

If she had simply ignored him, walked away…but she hadn't and now she was paying for her youthful temper.

Penelope released a long sigh and knew the PI was watching her, trying to read her expressions. Would KJ think her strange if she told her that her sixth sense was screaming, that there was something in the air, something brewing? That she knew her life was about to take a one-eighty turn?

She didn't want anything to change because change was terrifying. But a small part of her wanted her son to acknowledge her. An even tinier part of her wanted to tell him, and the world, who his father was, to allow the truth to spill out and move the hell on. But circumstances had recently changed and she needed to look at all the angles again.

KJ spoke again. "If there is anything else, any other way I can help you, will you let me know?"

She wished there was, but Penelope knew they'd hit a stone wall. Trouble was coming and there was nothing she could do to dissolve or divert it. She just had to deal with it when it happened. And hoped she, and her family, came out unscathed.

The chances of that happening were slim.

"I'll contact you when the lawyers contact me," KJ told her.

When… Penelope appreciated her optimism, but knew they wouldn't reach out. All the power lay with her son and it was his choice to use it or not.

All she could do was wait. And worry.

None of the Ryder-White family—except for Callum, who was still in the hospital—were happy with him, Cody decided later that day. He'd been avoiding James, refusing to talk to Kinga and Jules and ducking calls from Penelope. They'd all made it clear they wished to discuss Tinsley's broken heart. He didn't believe her heart was broken.

His, on the other hand, was close to snapping.

He'd never felt so—damn, this was difficult to admit—*lost* in his life. And he couldn't understand why. His life was mostly back to the way it had been before their encounter on New Year's Eve.

Encounter?

That was one way to put it. Another would be to call that night the six hours that rocked his world and changed his life.

Cody, still in his suit, stood by the huge bi-fold doors that separated his living room from the balcony and looked out onto the dark, clear night. He held a glass of whiskey in his hand, but he'd drunk little of it. Mostly because he thought that if he started, he might not stop.

Two weeks had passed since he'd last seen her and not having Tinsley in his life was becoming more difficult to deal with, not easier. In this case, time wasn't his friend. With every day that passed, the realization that their split might be permanent, that she genuinely didn't want to be with him, seemed to sink a little deeper into his psyche.

Cody felt himself shutting down, like he had when his mom died, remembering how desperate he felt as he came to realize his father wasn't going to step up to the plate and be the dad he needed. That he was alone and responsible for his genius brother.

God, he no longer wanted to feel alone.

He wanted to be with Tinsley, to create the family with her he'd only recently realized he wanted.

Cody heard his front door open, frowned and cocked his head to the side. He heard the sound of a bag hitting the floor and the door slamming closed. He had a baseball bat in the hallway closet, but that wouldn't help him now; he was too far away. His eyes darted around the room, looking for a weapon, and he stealthily walked across the room to pick up an exceptionally heavy glass vase.

"Are you going to brain me with that?"

He heard her voice and couldn't understand why Tinsley was standing at the entrance to his sitting room, dressed in tight jeans, those knee-high boots

JOSS WOOD   209

he loved and a short, bright berry-colored sweater worn under a leather jacket. What the hell was she doing here?

He took in her pink nose, her tousled hair and her always lovely face. She looked so much better than she had when he'd last seen her at the doctor's office, a lifetime ago. She looked vibrant, gorgeous, alive…damn near perfect.

And she was here, in his friggin' apartment!

"Can you put that vase down, Cody?"

Cody frowned and realized he was holding the vase above his head. He lowered the vase, replaced it on the mantel and, with his back to her, gathered his thoughts. Why was she here? What did she want? And why did she have her favorite overnight bag?

"If you've come for a quick bang, you can walk right on out," he muttered, his voice sharp. He whirled around and glared at her. "And how the hell did you get in here? I never authorized my private elevator to let you up."

"I know the codes to both the elevator and the front door, Cody," Tinsley softly replied, jamming her hands in the back pockets of her jeans. "You gave them to me."

"And that just shows you how stupid I can be!"

Tinsley gestured to the sofa. "Can I come in and sit down or do you want me to leave?"

Cody hauled in a deep breath, thought of telling her to leave and then waved in the direction of the couch. "Sit. Do you want something to drink?"

"A glass of red wine would be nice."

Cody started to tell her that she couldn't have wine, and then snapped his jaw closed so hard he was sure he cracked a tooth. She wasn't pregnant, he reminded himself. She could drink wine, eat shellfish, go scuba diving if she wanted to.

He'd finally embraced the idea of being a dad, only to have it ripped away from him. It hurt...but not as much as it did to lose Tinsley.

Swallowing hard, Cody met her eyes and saw understanding there, the flash of deep sadness. She handed him a tiny shrug and released a wobbly sigh.

Needing to do something with his hands, Cody walked into his kitchen, opened his wine cabinet and pulled out the first bottle of red he saw. He found a corkscrew, pulled the cork and dashed the liquid into a wineglass. With jerky steps, and his ears up around his shoulders, he walked back to her, shoving the glass into her hand.

"Why are you here, Tinsley? It can't be for business as we've been exchanging oh-so-polite emails for the past few weeks."

Tinsley placed her wineglass on the coffee table, its contents untouched. She crossed her legs and linked her hands around her knees and Cody remembered how she'd remove her boots and tuck her feet up under her butt. But this wasn't a social call.

He had no idea what it was...

Before he could ask again, Tinsley leaned forward and clasped her hands, holding them between her knees. "As you've told me, on more than one occasion, I have control issues," Tinsley said, her eyes clashing with his. Without dropping his gaze, he sat down in the chair opposite her, arms on his bouncing knees.

"I've only just figured out why I need to be perfect, why it's so important to me," Tinsley admitted.

He cocked his head, silently asking her to explain.

"When I was very young, eight or so, I overheard a conversation between Callum and my dad. I've only just accepted what impact Callum's comment had on my life. He'd told my dad that Kinga and I needed to be perfect or else my dad would suffer. And that seeded my need for perfection. I'm controlling because I never think I am good enough, perfect enough."

He wanted to protest, to reassure her, but something in her face, deep in her eyes, had him holding back his words. She needed to get this out, he realized, and he needed to let her.

"Being controlling is like a quick hit, a fast high. At the moment, I feel reassured and strong, but it never lasts. It quickly fades and the anxiety returns. I've realized that the need for complete control, the quest for perfection, is like chasing mist. Life is uncertain and there are no guarantees,"

She was right about that. Life didn't hand out guarantees. He'd thought his sick mom would recover and be fine, that his dad would assume responsibility for them, but he'd been wrong on both counts.

"I stayed in a dead marriage because I thought that if I could make everything perfect, JT would love me. After the divorce, I micromanaged my life because I am so damn anxious about getting everything right," Tinsley continued, sounding sad. She looked at her hands, then at the floor.

"Underneath my quest for perfection is that eight-year-old me, flawed and looking for reassurance that I am enough, that I am loved. I thought that if I was a perfect little girl, Callum wouldn't punish my dad. I thought that if I made everything perfect for JT, he'd love me. I thought that if I was the perfect sister or friend or employee, I would be happy."

Oh, Tinsley, that was so much self-inflicted pressure.

Tinsley lifted her eyes and when all that deep blue met his gaze, Cody felt a fist in his solar plexus. "The thing is, around you, I never felt pressured to be anything other than the person I am, authentically me. With you, I felt—feel—like the best version of myself. Imperfect, so very imperfect, but *real*."

Her hand came out to take his and when their palms connected he felt love and warmth rush through him. He adored her, wanted her, loved her, but he also liked her. Really liked the funny, flawed person she was.

"I can be real with you. You demand it of me. I like who I am with you," Tinsley admitted. She pulled her bottom lip between her teeth and when she released it, he saw tiny tooth marks in the soft pink. He desperately wanted to kiss them away. "I was wrong not to tell you that I thought something was wrong with the baby, to try and go it alone. I should've told you about the doctor's appointment. I was so out of line and for that I apologize."

What else could he say but "Apology accepted"?

Tinsley's thumb brushed over his wrist and Cody felt heat skitter over his nerve endings. "I've missed you so much, Cody. Every day that we've been apart, I've wanted to be in your arms."

He couldn't allow himself to be swept away, to dream. Crashing back to reality hurt too damn much. "You just like the sex, Tins."

Tinsley shook her head. "No, I love the sex." She shrugged, her cheeks now a little pink. "I love the way you touch me, the way you kiss me… Being naked with you is so much fun."

"I can't have another fun-filled fling with you, Tinsley," Cody stated, his tone harsh. He reached for her wineglass and downed its contents, wondering where he was going to find the strength to let her go. But it was either everything or nothing…

"I agree," Tinsley quietly stated. "I don't want a fling either."

Cody rubbed his forehead with his fingertips. "I have no idea what point you are trying to make, Tins."

"I'm trying to tell you, very badly, that I'd like something more between us." When his head shot up and his eyes connected with hers, she quickly lifted her hands. "I'm not expecting you to agree, but I need to tell you that I think I'm in love with you, that you're the only guy who's ever got me, the one man I can see myself with for the rest of my life."

"What?"

Tinsley lurched to her feet, the color draining from her face. "Okay, obviously that thought horrifies you. Um…can you forget I said it? I really don't want to go back to sniping at you, Cody so could we, maybe, try to be friends?"

Friends? Definitely not. Not wanting to waste time by walking around the coffee table, Cody bounded across it, ignoring its protesting creak as it briefly held his weight. Reaching Tinsley, he grabbed her shoulders and bent his knees to look into her face.

"Are you proposing?" he demanded, joy flooding his system.

She wrinkled her nose. "Only if that's something you might be interested in. Not now… I mean, I know you're going to need some time to get used to the idea, to me—"

"Tins?"

"Yes?"

"Stop. Talking." To make sure she did as he asked, Cody put his finger to her lips. "Can I say something?" he asked.

She nodded, her eyes wide and purple blue.

"I love you. I am insanely, wonderfully, completely in love with you and I've been damn miserable without you. Yes, you are occasionally frustrating but then, so am I. But mostly you are wonderful and sweet and lovely and kind." He dropped a kiss on her nose, then her cheekbone. "Don't change, Tins. I love you just the way you are."

Tinsley pulled her head back to look at him, looking for something in his face or in his eyes. Holding her face in his hands, he kept his gaze steady and his voice calm. "I want to marry you, to live with you and work with you. I want to make babies with you."

"How many?" Tinsley asked, sounding bemused and a little wary. He couldn't blame her since pregnancy hadn't been a fun experience for her.

"We'll start with one and see how it goes," he said, smiling to remind her that he was teasing. "Two at least. And then we'll keep our options open."

Then he remembered that he'd have to watch her suffer. Nope, he didn't think he could do it.

"No, wait, that won't work!" he said, shaking his head.

Tinsley looked crushed. "You've changed your mind about having babies?"

"No, I just can't watch you go through hell again, Tins. Can't we use a surrogate or something?"

Tinsley's eyes turned brighter, and her bottom lip wobbled. "That's the sweetest thing—apart from you telling me that you love me—I've ever heard." She lifted her hand to touch his cheek. "But do you know what? I would walk through hell time and time again to carry your baby, our baby. There's nothing I can't do without you next to me."

Her words filled up all those empty, blank spaces in his soul, filling them with light and warmth. "Does that mean you love me a little?"

"No, Cody, it means I love you with everything I have. You are everything I want. Your love is all that I will ever need."

That was all he needed to know. With a heart brimming over with love for this amazing woman, he pulled her into him, so her breasts rested against his chest, his arms around her. He smiled down at her. "Fair warning, you are going to need more than an overnight bag, sweetheart."

Tinsley grinned up at him. "I know." She almost wiggled with excitement. "I need to call the movers, tell my parents we're engaged—we are engaged, right?—call Kinga. And Jules… There's so much to do, Cody!"

Cody smiled, dropped a quick kiss on her lips and tipped her up and over his shoulder. "You can make a mental list until we hit the bedroom. When we get there, the only thing on your mind will be me." He squeezed her butt. "That work for you?"

Her hands caressed his back and Cody shuddered in anticipation. "*You* work for me, Gallant. I can't wait to spend the rest of my life with you, Cody."

Cody, hearing the emotion in her voice, lowered her to the bed and kissed her, a hot, needy, open-mouthed kiss, trying to show her how much he loved her. Tinsley moaned and returned his passion, tasting her love on his tongue, feeling it radiating from her skin.

Their one-night stand, Cody thought, was going to last the rest of the lives.

And that was the definition of perfection.

* * * * *

There's more Ryder-White drama to come!

Who will James select as the new Ryder CEO and will Penelope's secrets come to light? Will Garrett Kaye become part of the Ryder-White clan?

Read Garrett and Jules's story in the next novel in the Dynasties: DNA Dilemma series.

Lost and Found Heir

*To oust his twin brother from the family company,
CEO Samuel Kane sets him up to break the company's
cardinal rule—no workplace relationships. But it's Samuel
who finds himself tempted when Arlie Banks reawakens
a passion that could cost him everything...*

Read on for a sneak peek at
Corner Office Confessions
by USA TODAY *bestselling author Cynthia St. Aubin.*

A sharp rap on her door startled Arlie out of her misery.

"Just a minute!" she called, twisting off the shower.

Opening the shower door, she slid into one of the complimentary plush robes, then gathered the long skein of her hair and squeezed the water out of it with a towel before draping it over her shoulder.

Good enough for food delivery. She exited the bathroom in a cloud of steam and pulled open the propped door.

Samuel Kane's face appeared in the gap.

Only he didn't look like Samuel Kane.

He looked like wrath in a Brooks Brothers suit. Jaw set, the muscles flexed, mouth a thin, grim line. Eyes blazing emerald against chiseled cheekbones.

"Oh," she said dumbly. "Hi."

A sinking feeling of self-consciousness further heated her already shower-warmed skin as he stared at her.

"Do you want to come in?" she added when he made no reply. She stepped aside to grant him entry, catching the subtle scent of him as he moved past her into the hallway.

"Why didn't you tell me?" he asked.

Arlie's heart sank into her guts. There were too many answers to this question. And too many questions he didn't even know to ask.

"Tell you what?" she asked, opting for the safest path.

Coward.

Samuel stepped closer, her glowing white robe reflected in icy arcs in his glacier-green eyes. "About my father. About what he said to you this morning."

The wave of relief was so complete and acute it actually weakened her knees.

"Our families have a lot of shared history," Arlie said. "Not all of it good."

"He had no right—"

"I'm sorry," she interrupted, knowing it was a weak and deliberate dodge. She didn't want to talk about this. Not with him. "It's absolutely mandatory that you surrender your tie and suit jacket for this conversation. I'm entirely underdressed and frankly feeling a little vulnerable about it."

Walking into the well-appointed sitting area, Samuel shrugged out of his suit jacket and laid it across the chaise longue. As he turned, they snagged gazes. He gripped the knot of his tie, loosening it with small deliberate strokes that inexplicably kindled heat between Arlie's thighs.

"Better?" he asked.

On a different night, in a different universe, it would have ended there.

But for reasons she could neither explain nor ignore, Arlie padded barefoot across the space between them.

"Almost." Lifting her hands to his neck, she undid the button closest to his collar. Then another. And another.

To her great surprise and delight, Samuel wore no T-shirt beneath.

Dizzy with desire, Arlie tilted her face up to his. The air was alive with electricity, crackling and sizzling with anticipation. The breathless inevitability of this thing between them made her feel loose-limbed and drunk.

"All my life, I could have anything I wanted." Cupping her jaw, he ran the pad of his thumb over her lower lip. "Except you."

Arlie's breath came in irregular bursts, something deep inside her tightening at his admission. "You want me?"

Samuel only looked at her, silent but saying all.

His wordlessness the purest part of what he had always given her.

The look that passed between them was both question and answer.

Yes?

Yes.

Don't miss what happens next in...
Corner Office Confessions
by USA TODAY *bestselling author Cynthia St. Aubin.*

Available May 2022 wherever
Harlequin Desire books and ebooks are sold.

Harlequin.com

HDEXP0322

Get 4 FREE REWARDS!

We'll send you 2 FREE Books plus 2 FREE Mystery Gifts.

FREE Value Over **$20**

Both the **Harlequin® Desire** and **Harlequin Presents®** series feature compelling novels filled with passion, sensuality and intriguing scandals.

Love Harlequin romance?

DISCOVER.

Be the first to find out about promotions, news and exclusive content!

Facebook.com/HarlequinBooks

Twitter.com/HarlequinBooks

Instagram.com/HarlequinBooks

Pinterest.com/HarlequinBooks

YouTube.com/HarlequinBooks

ReaderService.com

EXPLORE.

Sign up for the Harlequin e-newsletter and download a free book from any series at **TryHarlequin.com**

CONNECT.

Join our Harlequin community to share your thoughts and connect with other romance readers!
Facebook.com/groups/HarlequinConnection

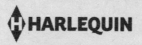

HSOCIAL2021

HARLEQUIN

Heartfelt or thrilling, passionate or uplifting—Harlequin is more than just happily-ever-after.

With twelve different series to choose from and new books available every month, you are sure to find stories that will move you, uplift you, inspire and delight you.